DREAMS OF
Glory

DREAMS OF
Glory

BY

JANET LAMBERT

Author of "Star-Spangled Summer"

DECORATIONS BY WOODI ISHMAEL

Image Cascade Publishing

www.ImageCascade.com

MANUFACTURED IN THE UNITED STATES
OF AMERICA

A hardcover edition of this book was originally published by E. P. Dutton & Co. It is here reprinted by arrangement with Mrs. Jeanne Ann Vanderhoef.

First *Image Cascade Publishing* edition published 2001.
Copyright renewed © 1970 by Jeanne Ann Vanderhoef.

Library of Congress Cataloging in Publication Data
Lambert, Janet, 1895–1973.
        Dreams of glory.

(Juvenile Girls)
Reprint. Originally published: New York: E. P. Dutton, 1942.

ISBN 978-1-930009-27-1

Books By Janet Lambert

PENNY PARRISH STORIES
Star Spangled Summer 1941
Dreams of Glory 1942
Glory Be! 1943
Up Goes the Curtain 1946
Practically Perfect 1947
The Reluctant Heart 1950
TIPPY PARRISH STORIES
Miss Tippy 1948
Little Miss Atlas 1949
Miss America 1951
Don't Cry Little Girl 1952
Rainbow After Rain 1953
Welcome Home, Mrs. Jordon
1953
Song in Their Hearts 1956
Here's Marny 1969
JORDON STORIES
Just Jennifer 1945
Friday's Child 1947
Confusion by Cupid 1950
A Dream for Susan 1954
Love Taps Gently 1955
Myself & I 1957
The Stars Hang High 1960
Wedding Bells 1961
A Bright Tomorrow 1965
**PARRI MACDONALD
STORIES**
Introducing Parri 1962
That's My Girl 1964
Stagestruck Parri 1966
My Davy 1968
CANDY KANE STORIES
Candy Kane 1943
Whoa, Matilda 1944
One for the Money 1946

DRIA MEREDITH STORIES
Star Dream 1951
Summer for Seven 1952
High Hurdles 1955
CAMPBELL STORIES
The Precious Days 1957
For Each Other 1959
Forever and Ever 1961
Five's a Crowd 1963
First of All 1966
The Odd Ones 1969
SUGAR BRADLEY STORIES
Sweet as Sugar 1967
Hi, Neighbor 1968
**CHRISTIE DRAYTON
STORIES**
Where the Heart Is 1948
Treasure Trouble 1949
**PATTY AND GINGER
STORIES**
We're Going Steady 1958
Boy Wanted 1959
Spring Fever 1960
Summer Madness 1962
Extra Special 1963
On Her Own 1964
**CINDA HOLLISTER
STORIES**
Cinda 1954
Fly Away Cinda 1956
Big Deal 1958
Triple Trouble 1965
Love to Spare 1967

Dear Readers:

Mother always said she wanted her books to be good enough to be found in someone's attic!

After all of these years, I find her stories—not in attics at all—but prominent in fans' bookcases just as mine are. It is so heart-warming to know that through these republications she will go on telling good stories and being there for her "girls," some of whom find no other place to turn.

With a heart full of love and pride–
Janet Lambert's daughter,
    Jeanne Ann Vanderhoef

TO

JEANNE ANN

CONTENTS

❦

DREAMS OF
Glory

★

CHAPTER I

WEST POINT WELCOME

"It looks fine, doesn't it?" Penny skipped across the rug, moved a chair a fraction of an inch, and surveyed the living room with satisfaction. "We're the world's fastest movers."

She flopped down into the chair, sighed happily and stretched her legs before her. Her brown curls were hot around her face, and she shoved them back with her arm as she grinned at her mother.

"We're always speedy," Mrs. Parrish laughed. "But we were never as quick as this. Really, Penny, you've hurried me until I'm exhausted." She, too, leaned her head against the restful back of a chair, and Penny's brown eyes danced as she looked at her.

"I know it." Penny bounced up to perch beside her mother. "But this is West Point, darling," she reminded her, as she patted her smooth cheek. "We never moved to West Point before. Why, just think how exciting it is. You can see your little boy, David, all the time—the whole six feet of him in his cadet uniform; you can go to New York whenever you like, to buy me beautiful evening gowns so that I can be the belle of the ball—the hop, I mean; and we can . . . Listen! I hear a car!"

She flew to the window, and after one hasty glance, was dashing across the room and through the hall. "It's Carrol!" she cried as she ran. "She's here!"

The screen door banged behind her and she hurtled toward a tall, slender girl who was standing in the drive. Chestnut curls were crushed against blond in a hurried embrace before brown eyes and blue began a swift appraisal.

"Well, Miss Houghton, you haven't changed a bit," Penny said with relief. "Except that, you're even prettier than you were last summer. Do you think I look older?"

"Not much." Carrol laughed as she looked at the gypsy sparkle that was Penny. "After all, it's only been a little over two months since I visited you at Fort Arden. You couldn't be very different, you know."

"Oh, but I am," Penny insisted. "I had to get the whole family moved; all by myself. Mummy was so excited about coming to be near David that she was no help at all, and Daddy just stayed over at the regiment; and Bobby kept bringing little boys home to play in the crates; and Tippy had to have her fourth birthday party. . . . Why, I aged ten years!" Penny paused for breath, saw the mirth in Carrol's eyes, and ended with another extravagant hug. "I did work hard," she said defensively. "I was so darned anxious to get here."

"I know it. And I thought you would never come." Carrol returned the embrace and added, "We lost the month you were to spend with Daddy and me, but this is much nicer than a visit. Why, Pen, just think, you're going to *live* here at West Point! We'll only be a few miles apart; and you can drive over to Gladstone Farms to see me. And when we move into New York for the winter, we'll have wonderful times. You Army people are so unpredictable," she analyzed. "You get nicely settled somewhere and then away you go. This time, I'm glad." She spied Mrs. Parrish on the steps and ran toward her. "Oh, Mrs. Parrish," she cried, "I can't believe it!"

"I can't either." Marjorie Parrish gave her a quick kiss and thought of the day on the hot station platform in Kansas, when first Penny had brought Carrol home to visit. She searched the happy face for some traces of the sadness and reserve it had held then, and was relieved when she found none. "How is your father?" she asked.

"Wonderful! Oh, Mrs. Parrish," Carrol's eyes brimmed with gratitude, "we have such *wonderful* times together. Daddy is the one perfect man in the world; though he says he's still trying to copy Major Parrish. He says he can't see why he ever let me spend all those years at Grandmother's. He's spoiling me terribly."

"I'm glad of that; and it won't hurt you a bit." Again Mrs. Parrish's mind flashed back, and she saw the frigid man Penny had inveigled into a visit. Langdon Houghton had had time to amass a great fortune in New York, but no time for his motherless little daughter, who lived with her grandmother in Chicago. Penny's plans, and Penny's absurd but grim determination that he should spend a week with them; should learn to know and love his daughter and, like a knight in a fairy tale, should rescue her from a lonely life, had brought amazing results. He had turned into the most human of human beings; and Carrol had been whisked away with him. Now, the future held a bright promise of companionship with the finest friend the Parrishes had even known. She looked at Penny, jigging excitedly from one foot to the other, and suggested: "Shall we go in and see our establishment?"

"Let's." Penny grabbed Carrol's hand and pulled at the door. "It's kind of different from the big old house at Arden," she rattled on, "but it's nice, and very elegant. No porch, you see, but we have a sun room."

"I miss your wonderful porch." Carrol smiled at Marjorie Parrish, and felt completely at home in these strange surroundings when the gay, answering dimples flashed a welcome to her.

"This is the hall," Penny was saying in so matter-of-fact a tone that they both looked around them in surprise.

"Are you *sure?*" Carrol asked, peering at the stairway. "Isn't it the kitchen?"

"Silly." Penny led the way into a long living room and waved her hand. "Living room here; sun room just beyond. Dining room across the hall, with breakfast room and kitchen behind. Upstairs four bedrooms, two baths, with the garage hooked onto the house."

Carrol walked into the living room and studied its long length. The grand piano fitted comfortably into its strange corner and the tables and chairs were as inviting in their new arrangement as they had been in the rambling old house at Fort Arden. The silver horse Major Parrish had won in a never-to-be-forgotten horse show, stood proudly on the mantel; and the sun room was gay with chintz.

"When the Parrishes move," she said shyly to Penny's mother, "they bring their whole world with them. I'd know this was your house even if I couldn't see you in it. It looks so happy."

"Thank you, dear." Mrs. Parrish gave her a quick pat and turned her head toward the hall. "I think I hear more of the welcoming committee coming."

There was a clatter, followed by shrieks; and Carrol found her knees in the embrace of a miniature Bo Peep, while her ears rang from the yells of a small cowboy. She hugged the children to her, set Tippy's muslin hat straight above her curls and tweaked Bobby's red neck-scarf.

"I believe they've grown," she said when her voice could be heard above their chatter. "Do they like it here?"

"They sho' does." The voice from the door brought her to her feet and, with a push for her ardent admirers, she sprang toward the little colored woman who was standing there.

"Trudy!"

"Yas'm, it's me." Trudy held out her hands and Carrol clasped them. "Miss Carrol, honey, yo' gets beautifuller and beautifuller. Let's look at yo'." The eyes of the faithful family servant and guardian of the young Parrishes from babyhood, traveled over Carrol; from her honey-colored curls, her patrician face with its endearing dimple at the corner of the mouth, to her soft blue sport suit and her polished brogues. Then she glanced at Penny. "Yo' sho' looks undressed-like in them shorts, Miss Penny," she commented dryly.

"I know it." Penny smoothed her wrinkled shirt and grinned engagingly. "But I'm a working woman. I'll change right away. I'll put on my new pink-plaid blanket skirt and my wine jacket," she exulted. She flew up the stairs and in a surprisingly short time skipped down again, her neat page-boy bob topping her newest ensemble.

"Think I'll knock the cadets dead?" she asked as she posed in the door.

"Are we going . . . ?" Carrol stopped and blushed, but Penny grinned and finished the sentence for her.

"Sure. We're going over to Grant Hall and call David out. He's through his afternoon classes now." She waved the hopeful Bobby and Tippy back and turned to her mother. "Want to come, too, Mums?"

"No, thank you, darling. I'll find the orderly and have Carrol's bag brought in. You *are* spending the night, aren't you, dear?"

"I'd like to, thank you; and I brought some clothes. But Daddy will be over after dinner and I'll have to see if he can spare me. He went in to New York on business, but said he'd hurry as fast as he could."

"Good. Now run along—and give my son my love."

As they got into the car, Penny looked at Carrol with admiration. "Did you drive all the way by yourself?" she wondered.

"Of course," Carrol answered with a laugh. "I'm sixteen now, you know, and Daddy gave me the car for my birthday."

"Gosh." Penny ran her hand over the smooth red leather of the smart convertible and looked at Carrol in awe. "I'll be fifteen next week but I don't see any car in the offing; or even a chance to drive the good old family sedan. There are always too many people wanting it."

"We won't need it." Carrol flipped the switch. "We have this one. Do you remember how we talked last summer about having one all our own? Oh, Penny, now we have it! And we're going to be near each other all winter, and . . ." she turned eagerly to Penny . . . "tell me, does David look just the same?"

"Oh, sure." Penny considered David in a sisterly fashion and added, "His uniform makes him look even taller and slimmer and older—but you'll see when we get there."

Carrol hoped she would; and as they rolled along, she saw a great many other things that Penny pointed out. There were hillsides dotted with officers' brick homes; a section for the younger married couples, that looked like a toy village in the distance; and the gray and historic buildings that were the Military Academy, itself. Its quadrangle of barracks fronted the drill field; a shaded walk and benches provided comfort for spectators who came to watch the corps of eighteen hundred marching cadets; and from it, winding roads toiled up into the hills or disappeared over the cliff.

"The whole place is just up or down," Penny explained unnecessarily. "And, as the cadets have no transportation, I've nearly walked myself to death. The athletic field is way down there," her finger zig-zagged through a park with monuments and cannon, bent like a melted candle, then jerked upward again, "and the chapel's way up on top."

Carrol's eyes lifted to the beautiful stone church, only to be drawn down again toward a hidden riding hall and the broad, swift Hudson River. Penny's finger flipped about, and academic buildings and officers' club, the General's house, the hospital and several Halls were ticked off so rapidly that, from her recital, only a vague, fascinating panorama was clear.

"I'll straighten it out someday," Carrol laughed as she

parked the car. "Just now, I'm confused." She looked at the boys hurrying along the walk, stiff and erect in their gray uniforms, blouses buttoned under their chins. There were tall boys, short boys, thin ones and fat ones; but they were all dressed alike, from their military caps to their polished black shoes. David could be among them, she thought, and I'd probably not recognize him. Carrol followed Penny through the great doors of Grant Hall and envied the ease with which she sauntered to the desk where sat a busy cadet.

"Please call out Cadet Parrish, D.G.-Company A," Penny tossed off when he looked up. Then she returned to Carrol. "He's the junior officer of the guard," she explained. "And David is in A Company, which has the tallest boys. That's the Boodlers', in there," she added as they passed an open door. "It's like the Post Exchange soda fountain, and we'll go in as soon as David comes."

Carrol had a glimpse of closely packed tables and chairs surrounded by noisy young men, before Penny piloted her into a large reception room, comfortable with divans and chairs and lamps. They seated themselves sedately, but Penny, after a careful smoothing of her blanket-plaid skirt, bounced about on her cushion and launched into a vivid description of her week-old life at the Point.

"It's dull during the week, and I don't know any of the upper classmen yet," she confided. "The plebes—they're the freshmen like David—can't do any of the exciting things. They can't go to the hops or along Flirtation Walk; but it will be fun, anyway."

"David wrote that he would get us dates for the hops whenever we wanted to go," Carrol interjected. "He said that some of the yearlings have 'recognized' him."

"They have? Well, fancy that!" Penny wriggled with joy. "They don't have to. You know, I thought they wouldn't speak to him for a whole year. Wouldn't it be *awful*," she whispered, her eye on a cadet who was boredly showing a relative around, "to be a poor little plebe and have boys you've known all your life walk right by you without speaking? I don't think I could stand the things the upper classmen do to them."

"I couldn't, either." Carrol's heart skipped a beat, for David, cap in hand, was standing in the door. David. Just as he had looked last June. Blond hair brushed smooth, blue eyes twinkling, and firm lips quirked upward in a grin.

"Hi!"

"Hi, yourself. And look what I've brought." Penny jumped up, and Carrol found her hand in a strong, hard grip.

"Hello, David."

"Hello, Carrol." He smiled down at her, then took the place Penny had vacated, leaving her to teeter on the sofa's arm. "Here we are."

"Umhum. Isn't it wonderful? I never thought it would come true, did you?"

"Well, I had hopes." He leaned back, and the three-sided conversation brought so many inquiring heads inside the door, that at last he looked up. "The word seems to have spread that there are two good-looking femmes in here, so it won't be long until you're on exhibition. I wish I could buy you a drink, but I'm not allowed in the Boodlers'."

"Oh, David, I forgot about that." Penny groaned in disappointment. "I wish you would get past being a plebe."

Her face cleared as other outcasts of the fourth class, seemingly intent on a thorough inspection of the reception room, found it necessary to consult David on questions of math, his health, or anything that came into their minds. He introduced them to the girls, then grinned ruefully as they collected chairs and turned the threesome into a party.

Penny was in her element. She chattered happily and was loath to leave when the general exodus for supper formation began; but was pacified by the gray squad that escorted her to the curb. She glanced back at Carrol and David on the steps and knew that David was making the most of his last hurried minutes.

"Thanks, Carrol, for writing so often," David was saying. "It was pretty hard going at first, and your letters helped a lot."

"I'm glad, David; and I loved having yours, too. Can't you ever come down to visit?"

"Nope. But we've got the football game in New York to look forward to, and you'll come up here. Shall I see you tomorrow?"

"I don't know. I may have to go home."

"Well, try to stay. I get a half hour off and I'll lope over home. Okay?"

"Okay." She smiled as he settled his movie tickets, his handkerchief and an odd assortment of trifles in his cap that served for pockets.

"Watch this," he said as he set it firmly on his head and threw back his shoulders. "Watch Cadet Parrish, D.G. strut his stuff."

Her eyes followed him as he strode away and when she joined Penny she shook her head. "David was always straight," she grumbled. "Now he looks as though he had a poker down his back."

"West Point training, my dear." Penny grimaced as she got into the car. "And David wants it. Let's hustle home and see if Dad is there."

A long black limousine blocked the drive when they drew up and Carrol slammed on her brake. "Your father has come!" Penny cried. "And our car is in the garage. Oh, hurry!"

They rushed up the walk, waving as they ran, and calling to the two men who were standing in the door. One, in uniform and polished boots, was an older duplicate of David, and he held out his arms to Carrol. The other, tall and darkly handsome, steadied himself for the rushing Penny and swung her up to kiss her.

"Well, my Good Fairy," he laughed as he set her down, "I see you got here."

"I certainly did. Hi, Daddy." She gave her father a pat, then gathered them all into her embrace. "Isn't it marvelous?" she cried. "Isn't it just too, too *marvelous?*"

They assured her that it was—even to Bobby and Tippy and her mother who came to join in the excitement, and she beamed on them.

"We're all here together!" she cried. "Just like we wanted to be."

There was a scratching on the screen, and she turned to look into the imploring eyes of a gangling police pup. "Yes sir," she laughed as she threw the door wide for him, "we're all here—even to Woofy."

CHAPTER II

GLADSTONE FARMS

The September sunshine was warm as Penny and Carrol ticked off the miles to Gladstone Farms. "It really isn't very far," Carrol said. "And I'm glad now that Daddy sold the Connecticut place and bought this one. We like it better, and it's so much nearer you. Do you know where you'll go to school, Pen?"

"Briarcliff, probably," Penny answered without enthusiasm. "Oh, dear." She switched off the radio and faced Carrol. "You'll be moving to New York the first of October and we'll both be in school. We'll have to crowd in all the fun we can before then."

"I know it. But we'll be out at Gladstone every week-end, or you can come to town. It won't be bad." Carrol eased the car around a truck and motioned across the hills that were still green, but appeared lazy and somnolent, as though napping in the warmth before blazing into a final barrage of color. "That's Gladstone, over there."

"It is? So soon?" Penny leaned forward eagerly and in a few moments was peering through the windshield. "It's darling," she said, as great stone gates gave a view of a small, gabled cottage. "Aren't you going to stop?"

Carrol had swung the car into the drive and was waving to a child who smiled up at her. "That's the lodge house," she explained. "The head gardener lives there to see that the gates are locked at night. Our house is farther in."

"Oh." Penny's eyes searched the woodland as the drive wound on and on, and when an English manor house came into view, she gasped. The lower half of the house was brick; its upper, white stucco with dark-stained beams; and it stretched before her like a castle. The center section curved in an arc, and turrets divided it from long wings on either end. A haughty, semi-circular terrace warded off the drive-way, and chairs and gay umbrellas were dwarfed by the tall French windows behind them. "My goodness," she gasped, "I thought you had a farm house."

"I know you did." Carrol laughed and stopped the car. "I wanted to see your face when you got a view of this. I hope you're impressed."

"Impressed! I'm practically knocked unconscious." They began to giggle, and Penny leaned out to look at the house again. "It's sumpin'," she said with a shake of her head. "I feel like little Lord Fauntleroy. Dashed if I don't! All we need now is the grandfather." At her words, an elderly man in cutaway with striped trousers came onto the terrace. "Is he the earl?"

"He's the butler." Carrol climbed out of the car and came around to the still blinking Penny. "He's a nice old thing, really, even though he does look so pompous. You know, Daddy goes in for a great deal of style."

"I can see he does," Penny murmured as she followed Carrol into the house and managed a smile for Perkins, the butler. "I should have known it from his private planes and valets. It was just the word 'farms' that misled me." She looked around her in pleased content. "This place is big enough for a hotel—but I have a feeling that I'm going to like it."

She skipped from room to room, was fascinated by the wing her family was to have when they came to visit, and dashed about the bedroom and sitting room that she and Carrol would share.

"Look, Penny," Carrol pointed out. "My drapes are pink like yours and my rug is rose."

"So they are, pet." Penny rushed across the room, curls flying, and gave Carrol a hasty squeeze. "I have to see everything!" she cried. "I never was so excited in my life."

She chattered all the way down the broad stairway and toured the lower rooms like a happy puppy in a new home. "After I've looked it all over and got the lay of the land, as you might say, I'll know where I'm going—but just now, it's a maze. Game room, morning room, sun room, library, drawing-room. . . . Oh, Carrol!" She broke off to tiptoe across the drawing-room and stand silently before a portrait that caught the late afternoon rays of the sun.

"It's Mother," Carrol said softly, as she followed her.

"I know." Penny's eyes were filled with tears. "She was so beautiful." Her hand reached for Carrol's as she smiled up at the lovely girl above them. "We're very happy," she told her simply. "Thank you, so much."

Then she whirled Carrol around and they went out into the sunshine.

"What do we do next?" she asked, as she looked across the wide lawn that was shaded by elms, gray and old and towering.

"Well, we could see the badminton and tennis courts. They're over this way."

They walked through a garden that was walled from view by pointed evergreens. Its path, seemingly haphazard, led to more bright furniture and more striped umbrellas, and to the blue-green water of the swimming pool.

At every new sight Penny became more sober. And as they strolled along a lane that turned and twisted beside a companionable little brook, she was very quiet. The lane ended at broad stable doors, but the brook bubbled on like a happy tourist; and she stood watching it.

"What is it, Pen?" Carrol asked. "I never knew you to be so silent."

"I know it. I was thinking about you," she answered as she sat down against a tree. "How you have all this—and yet you aren't silly or important or trying to put on airs."

"For goodness' sake, why should I, Pen?" Carrol's blue eyes widened with surprise. "I told you, last summer, that I've always had more money than I knew what to do with— but I'd never had love. All Daddy gave me was money. Now, he's giving me love, too. And that's more important to me than all the swimming pools and cars in the world. I wouldn't have that, but for you."

"Maybe not." Penny looked off into space and sighed. "We haven't quite got at what I'm feeling," she said at last. "Maybe I don't know what it is, myself. I'll ask Mummy; she'll know. And in the meantime, let's forget it." She jumped up and ran into the stable, a chattering, laughing Penny again.

"This is Martinette," Carrol said, as a black thoroughbred looked over her stall into the broad center aisle of the stable.

"She's as nearly like your beloved Tango Dance as Daddy and I could find. And see, we have Floridian, because he looks like my precious Ragamuffin. Was Ragamuffin all right when you left Arden, Pen?"

"He was fine—but he said he missed you." Penny stroked Martinette and laid her face against the cool muzzle. "Let's go riding soon."

"All right. And we have bicycles, too. They're in the garage. Want to look?"

"Let's. It will be wonderful to go zooming around the country on our bikes. Do you know what I'd like to do?"

She launched into a whirlwind of plans that lasted through the inspection of the bicycles, a station wagon, a limousine and the greenhouses, and they were months ahead in their plans when they reached the house again.

"There is a letter for you, Miss Carrol," a trim little maid said, as the girls came into the book-lined library. "It came yesterday."

Carrol took the letter and looked at the return address on the back. "Good grief," she exclaimed to Penny, "it's from Louise!"

"From *Louise?* For goodness' sake, open it!"

They rushed to the divan, fell onto it, and both heads bent over as Carrol slit the flap. Penny gave one look at the flourishing handwriting that covered the page and leaned back. "You read it aloud," she said in disgust. "It's the craziest-looking scrawl I ever saw."

Carrol scanned the words for some semblance to consonants and vowels, then began to decipher: "*Carrol dearest*," she read.

" 'Carrol dearest,' " Penny muttered. "Now, isn't that just like her!—after the way she treated you at Arden? Go on."

"I'm so sorry I didn't see you after your accident. I do feel a little to blame for it . . ."

"A *little* to blame," Penny interrupted again. "That girl!

Her horse just kicks yours into a cocked hat and knocks you off and busts your head wide open—and she feels 'a little to blame'! Well, struggle on again. I'll try to contain myself."

"And I can't tell you how unhappy I have been over it. What?"

"I just said, that's something, anyway. Carry on." Penny slid down on her spine and Carrol puzzled out the words.

"Mother brought me east to school and I'm staying with my aunt until Seaton Seminary opens. I do so much want to see you, and I'd ask you here but it is rather boring, as my aunt is slightly ancient. I'm going up to the Point next week-end, dragging Michael Drayton . . .'"

"WhoOOOO?" Penny sat up with a bounce and her voice crescendoed in a shriek. "Over my dead body is she dragging Michael! Let me see that thing." She took the letter, stared at it, then shook it. "Now listen here, Miss Frazier," she told it, "you of the black hair and the long, twining eyelashes, Cadet Drayton is all sewed up with me next week, so keep your little paws off. I'll bet she hasn't even written Mike she's coming," she stormed. "What's the matter with Dick dragging her? Do you suppose he's stopped mooning about her since he got in the Point?"

"Well, I hope he has. Dick Ford acted like an idiot last summer."

"You'd better not hope so, my little 'Carrol dearest.'" Penny wagged her head. "Or you'll find her making life miserable for David again and pursuing Mike. Go on and finish." She tossed Carrol the letter. "I guess I can bear up for a few more shocks."

"There isn't much more. She just says she wants to see me at the Point, and signs it 'lovingly, Louise.'"

"'Lovingly, Louise!' Oh me, oh my." Penny made a face, then laughed. "The girl certainly gets in my hair," she apologized, "but every time I think of that moonlight picnic and you ending up in the hospital, I see red. What *I* see, though, is pale pink beside what David sees. What are we going to do about her?"

"What is there to do, Penny? I wouldn't be here now if I hadn't fallen off of my horse and cut my head and frightened Daddy so badly; and I wouldn't have fallen off if Clip Along hadn't kicked Ragamuffin. So I really don't feel badly toward her. I don't believe she'll be unpleasant any more."

"Well, I do. She's after Mike now—and I like Mike."

"Pen, Mike has more sense than to fall for Louise. She won't go after those boys who were at Arden. Wait and see. She'll only ask them to introduce her to other cadets."

"Maybe so." Penny looked down at the letter. "But she'll drape herself around our necks, and I don't want her. She was so jealous of you, and so horrid to you, all last summer, because you had lots of money and because you were visiting David and me. Now she wants to visit you."

"Well, I hope she never will. So let's forget her. She hasn't a date with Mike and I think it will be rather fun to wait and see what she does. How about a little tennis?"

"All right." Penny looked dolefully at Carrol. "I have so many troubles," she sighed. "First it's Louise—and now you're going to run me to death—and then win every game from me."

★

ENTER LOUISE

The days flew by, and it was Saturday afternoon before Penny had an opportunity to discuss her problems with her mother. Finding her in the sun room ministering to a tired begonia plant, Penny threw herself into a chair and came straight to the point.

"I've got a worry, Mums," she began, "and it bothers me."

"You have, darling? What is it?" Her mother set the begonia on the window sill and came to give Penny her undivided attention.

"Well. . . ." Penny studied her shoes and shook her head. "It's hard to explain. When Carrol first began to show me Gladstone I was terribly impressed. The more I saw, the tennis courts and the swimming pool and a garage that's bigger than our house, and stables that are paneled in pine, I got over being awed—and kind of wanted to own it. Carrol pressed little buttons and servants came running and . . . Mums, she didn't seem to think much about it, but I wondered if I would be satisfied now—just having a front yard and a back yard. I've never been jealous of Carrol . . ." She lifted troubled eyes to her mother. "You don't think I am, do you?"

"Penny," her mother smiled as she sat down, "you probably *are* a little envious, not jealous—just envious. It's the first time you have been out of your own little Army world. And Gladstone *is* lovely. But did you stop to weigh your family,

Daddy and me, and your brothers and little sister, against a life of just pushing buttons for servants?"

"Yes, I did." Penny was sober as she answered. "I wouldn't give up my family for all the big estates in the world, but . . . well, I wanted you and Gladstone, too."

"Just a Communist at heart."

The voice from the door was such a surprise that Penny and her mother looked around with a start. David was leaning against the frame and grinning. "Penny believes in the equal distribution of wealth," he teased.

"Oh, David, I don't. You haven't heard enough to get the point." Penny frowned at him, but he only tousled her hair and went over to kiss his mother.

"Sure you do." He sat down astride a chair and his grin was still broad as he looked at her over its back. "Mr. Houghton earned his house and Dad earns this one. Would you give up the Army to have the wide acres of Gladstone?"

"You know I wouldn't."

"Well, then, what are you crying about? No one person has everything—and did you ever stop to consider that Carrol might rather have what we have?" He leaned around the door and called: "Hey, Carrol. Come here. Trudy's teaching her to bake a swell-looking cake," he added, licking his lips.

Light footsteps sounded in the hall and Carrol came in, one of Trudy's big aprons tied around her waist. "Did I hear myself being paged?" she asked. Then she saw the family conference, and added: "Is something up?"

"Yeah." David took charge of the conversation again, while Penny looked murderously at him and his mother hid a smile. "Penny envies you Gladstone."

"I do not!" Penny shouted, forgetting that she did. "I just said . . ."

"Oh, Penny!" Carrol wiped a smudge of flour from her face with her apron and laughed. "You don't envy me a thing; and you know you don't. You just got dramatic from wandering around in the gardens, like you did the time you wanted to be Hedy Lamarr. You wouldn't trade places with anyone in the world."

"I know it." Penny flounced out of her chair. "But it seems to me that, in this family, a discussion of a fellow's personal feelings is about as private as a debate in Congress. I started out just talking to Mummy—and now look at the crowd I've collected."

"Well, you like to be the center of attention." David set his chair against the wall and sniffed a fragrant odor that was wafting in from the kitchen. "Besides, the conference will do you good. Did you ever have a boil?" He followed Carrol to the door and, without waiting for Penny's mute nod, added, "If you have, you know that the quickest way to cure it is to let the poison out. Am I right, Mums?"

Mrs. Parrish winked at him and returned to her begonia; and Penny smiled. "I have been properly spanked," she said. Then she hung her head and twisted her toe into the rug, in comic imitation of Tippy. "Penny is a good girl now," she lisped. "Please, may I have a piece of cake?"

"You may not. But you can look at it." Carrol started to the kitchen as the doorbell rang.

Two cadet uniforms were visible through the glass and Penny sped to the door. "It's Dick and Michael," she called over her shoulder. "Thank goodness, they didn't get here in time to help rake me over the coals." She flung the door open and the hall was filled with shouts of welcome.

"You're a swell bunch," Dick chided, his broad face beaming and his red hair springing from the cap he tossed to Penny. "Not once have you ever come over and called us out. We could have died and you'd never have known it. Isn't that right, Mike?"

"That's right." Michael, darkly handsome, smoothed his black hair neat and smiled into the sun room. "Hello, Mrs.

Parrish," he said, going in to shake hands with her. "It's grand that you can be here with Dave."

"Isn't it wonderful? I hope you boys will come over often."

"You needn't worry about that, now that we've found the way." Dick, holding out his hand, too, abruptly knelt down and felt the rug. "Look, Mike," he exclaimed. "Real honest to gosh rugs! Feel 'em. And upholstered chairs!" He eased himself onto a down cushion, and a beatific smile spread across his face. "Boy, it feels good after nearly three months of barracks."

Penny fluttered about, and Mrs. Parrish went with Carrol to see about her cake. When Carrol returned with it on a plate, the welcoming shouts were a tribute to success; and Trudy, following with hot chocolate, hastily planned another dessert for dinner.

"It's like old times," Penny said as she leaned back against the pillows of a bamboo divan. "If only we had Mary and Jane and Bob . . ." She stopped, blushed with embarrassment, and added weakly, "and—and Louise."

"Oh, yes, dear Louise," Dick filled in, as her voice trailed off for lack of words. "We certainly should have Louise."

"What happened to you, Dick?" David asked curiously. "What made you stop carrying the torch for her?"

"I grew up." Dick considered the cake plate again, then compromised with his conscience by breaking a piece in half. "Little girls who can't shoot square aren't in my line."

"Did you tell her so?"

"You bet I told her." Dick looked at Michael and took a large bite of cake. "She's trying to cry on Mike's shoulder, now," he said through the crumbs.

"Got a date with her for the week-end, Mike?" David asked the question idly, but Penny saw the interest in his eyes and wondered if Carrol had told him about the letter. She listened eagerly for his answer and when it came, wished that she could purr.

"I have not. As nearly as our bunch ever dates, I'm dragging Pen. Louise wrote me that she'd like to join the crowd, but I got her a drag with the worst drip in our company, because I figured that that would put her in with her own kind. She can't bother us, then."

The telephone rang, and Penny, answering on the downstairs connection, heard her mother's voice on the one above.

"Who says Louise can't bother us?" she demanded as she returned to the sun room. "She's going to be right here with us."

"She *is?*" The chorus that answered her gave her ample encouragement for her histrionic ability, so she launched forth.

"Her aunt just called. They've driven over and she can't find a place where she can leave Louise for the week-end—not and feel safe about her, y'know. And so—would *deah* Mrs. Parrish take her in? It would be so-o-o sweet of her. *Deah* Mrs. Parrish was sweet, bless her noble heart—and we've got her. She's practically here."

"She is? Well, it was nice to have known you—and good-by." Dick jumped up, and with Michael and David behind him, dashed for the hall.

"You can't go and leave us!" Penny wailed, as she and Carrol rushed after them. "We haven't seen her since you have—not since she knocked Carrol off her horse, and it's going to be awful. I think you should stay and help us."

"Maybe we should." Michael looked at Penny's distressed face, then turned from her to David. "What do you think, Dave?"

"Gosh." David went to the foot of the stairs. "Hey, Mums," he called. "What's all this about Louise coming here?"

"Oh, David." Mrs. Parrish sat on the top step and looked down at the upturned faces. "I really couldn't help it. I couldn't think of an excuse to make. Trudy's flapping sheets in the guest room and muttering, and I feel like an outcast." She looked so doleful that the five below had to laugh.

"Well, we'll help the girls bear up for a little while," David offered grudgingly. "But we can't stay much longer." He looked at Penny. "Is she your guest?" he asked.

"She most certainly is not!" Penny was vehement in her denial.

"Do you want her, Carrol?"

"Not particularly."

"Somebody's going to have to entertain her." He looked up at his mother huddled on her step, and scowled. "It looks as though she's all yours, Mrs. Parrish," he said sternly. "All you have to do is to keep her out of our way. I hope this will be a lesson to you."

"Oh, it will, sir; indeed it will." Marjorie Parrish nodded forlornly, before her voice took on a more hopeful tone. "But you'll see that she has dates, won't you?"

"Oh, we'll get her dates." Because she looked so uncertain and much too young to have grown children teasing her, Michael came to her aid. "I have that all fixed up."

"Well, then, what's there to worry about?"

She scurried back to her sleeping arrangements before they could answer, and her disgruntled tormentors filed into the living room. There they waited with ill-concealed impatience for the moment when the doorbell should destroy their peace, and when a car door slammed they cringed, shuddered and moaned simultaneously.

"Uh-oh," David said, as Trudy pattered down the stairs, a reluctant reception committee of one. "She's right on time."

Louise came in like a breeze. Exclaiming, kissing, and fluttering her incredible eyelashes, she greeted them all. And the boys who were not physically embraced, were wrapped in a soft wooly blanket of smiles.

"Hello," she bubbled. "Dick and Michael! How wonderful! And David! Oh, bless your hearts, all of you. Carrol, I'm so thankful you're all right. Why, the scar doesn't even show. From all the reports I had, I thought you must look a sight—

but it just shows how people exaggerate, doesn't it?" She lifted her shoulders in the shrug she considered appealing and David winced in well-remembered irritation.

Penny stood stolidly to one side, braced for her turn, and when it came, was as responsive as a totem pole. "Hello," she welcomed sparingly. "Did your aunt come with you?"

"Oh, no, she's gone." Louise slid her arm around Carrol and assumed the pose of long-lost-but-united-at-last friendship. "I have a suitcase out on the grass," she said carelessly. "If one of you boys will trot it in . . ."

"We still have an orderly to bring it." Penny regretted that she had no buttons to push for service, and no Perkins to stalk impressively across the room. Usually, when she needed the colored soldier who acted as orderly she summoned him by shouting. But now, glad of a chance to leave the room, she went slowly down the basement stairs and spoke so softly that he looked up from his boot-polishing in surprise.

"Jumpin' Jiminy, Miss Penny, you gave me a start." He grinned at her, white teeth flashing. "Most always you go rompin' aroun' like a fire truck."

"I know it, Yates, but. . . ." Penny looked at him thoughtfully. "There's a suitcase out in the yard that has to be brought in. I don't suppose it could get misplaced or anything—no, I guess it couldn't. That wouldn't be quite fair."

"The Major says I'm awful forgetful." Yates had had a chat with Trudy, so he looked at her hopefully.

"You couldn't forget much—not from the driveway to the guestroom. Just dump the thing in. Trudy will unpack it."

She returned to her guests, only to find the boys sorting out their caps while Louise, at the hall mirror, did unnecessary things to her face. Carrol was perched on the bottom step of the stairway and her dimple flickered as she caught Penny's eye.

"Where are they all going?" Penny asked in surprise.

"Back to barracks." Carrol leaned against the wall and

added casually: "Louise asked if she could borrow my car to take them."

"Who's taking us where?" David took the cap that Dick held out and fitted it snugly on his head.

"I'm saving you a long walk, children." Louise twitched her hat into a saucy tilt as she turned from the mirror. "Carrol offered me her car and I'm going to drive you over to your little gray home. I haven't toured the Post myself, yet."

"Well, if there's any touring done, Carrol's going to do it." David took his cap off again and went to stand before Louise. He leaned his elbow on the newel post and five pairs of eyes were focused on him. At least four hearts did acrobatics and one, Penny's, pumped crazily with joy for the blow-up it hoped was coming.

"I don't know what the big idea is," David was saying, "but there's one thing we have to get straight around here. We used to be a good crowd. What one did, we all did. And that's the way it's got to be—if we stay a crowd, that is."

"I suppose you mean me," Louise answered with a toss of her head. "At least, you're looking at me. Just because the car won't hold us all . . ."

"I mean *all* of us. If you want to take what I'm going to say as a personal thing the rest of us can, too. There's been a lot of back-biting and jealousy and throat-cutting, and no crowd can stand up under it."

"I think you're perfectly insufferable, David Parrish." Louise's eyes blazed and she stamped her foot. "I know what you mean. You're just trying to get back at me because my horse bumped Carrol's."

"You know that isn't true." David's gaze was so steadfast and so honest that a little of the anger died out of her face. "If I do feel bitter, you might figure that you're some to blame, because you didn't even apologize after the accident— you just skipped off on a trip. I'm only trying to get us all straight again, like we used to be. I'm not blaming anybody or digging into the past—but I *am* saying, just as I told Penny this afternoon, that things don't heal until you get the poison out."

"He did say that, Louise, about me. He said . . ." Penny subsided as David shook his head at her, but the disappointment in her face brought a grin from Dick. Louise saw it and whirled on him.

"So you think I'm to blame for everything, too!"

Dick cut off his grin and searched for words, but David was into the breach before him.

"You've got it all wrong, Louise. I'm not talking about the past—it's gone. What I want us to do, is to forget it; to make up our minds that we'll be good sports and good friends in the present."

"The fine old West Point honor system, I suppose." Louise clipped out the words with a disdainful toss of her head, but realized her mistake as Dick's jolly face, for once, looked grim; and Michael, with a shrug, turned toward the door. "I'm sorry," she said hurriedly. She could see them all slipping away from her, and her eyes filled with tears. "I know it's been my fault. Daddy tried to sell Clip Along . . ." She sobbed, fumbled in her purse for a handkerchief, and turned her face to the wall.

Carrol sprang up but David blocked the way. "Save your tears for Clip Along," he said easily to Louise. "I wouldn't have the old goat on a bet, but you seem to love him. Let's just all try to remember what I've said—and let's be square with one another."

"I will, David." Louise whirled around, her lashes wet, her eyes misty and sad. "I've been pretty beastly in lots of ways. And I should have said, long ago, that I'm sorry." She turned to Carrol. "Really, I am, Carrol. I've been embarrassed about it and . . . well, I guess I've tried to bluff it out, because I didn't mean to do it."

"I know you didn't." Carrol pushed by David to put her

arm around Louise's sagging shoulders. "I've really been glad it happened because it gave me Daddy. But as David has said, we've all been at sword's points. So, let's don't be that way any more." She looked pleadingly at the boys until Michael, although he shook his head, came to give Louise a pat.

"Okay, Louise," he said. "We'll be the crowd again—thanks to David's good sense."

Penny, for whom pity could outweigh trust, doubt and judgment, all combined, entered heartily into the little group around Louise. At Dick's, "Gosh, we have to go," she bethought herself of her colleague in the basement and hurried down the stairs.

"Yates," she called from the bottom step, "is the suitcase upstairs?"

"Not yet, Miss Penny." A broom clattered to the floor and Yates' brown and grinning face peered at her around the furnace. "I cain' find it. It must of done get lost."

"Well, dig it out and shoot it into the guestroom. Everything's okay, now."

She flew back to join the crowd that was pouring out through the door, but stopped at a staccato of hisses that came from above.

"What was going on?" her mother asked, hanging perilously over the upstairs rail.

"We're all fixed up now. David did it." Penny waved and ran after the others. She climbed in beside Carrol and David and looked back at Louise, enthroned on the back seat between two uniforms.

Louise smiled at Dick and Michael alternately; appealing, wistful smiles, and her voice was plaintively subdued when she spoke. At her halting hopes for the week-end and her assurance to Michael that she was quite satisfied to spend it with "a drip," Dick nobly offered himself on the altar of sacrifice.

"You mean you'd really take me around, Dick? You *would?*" The glance she gave him was grateful, and tears quenched a sudden sparkle in her eyes. "It's awfully sweet of you."

"Glad to do it." Dick grinned uncomfortably, and welcomed the portals of Grant Hall with relief. "See you tonight."

The car lingered for farewells; moved a few feet and stopped for more last-minute conferences; then rolled on slowly.

"Want to climb up in front, Louise?" Penny asked as she slid over to make room.

"No thanks. It isn't worth while to change." Louise leaned back against the red leather and looked at the two heads in front of her. Her lips curved in the thinnest of smiles—and the little flame in her eyes that had been quenched, leaped out again.

CHAPTER IV

NEW YORK, AT LAST

The forty-eight hours of Louise's hampering presence loomed ahead like a hill that seems straight and steep in the distance. But wheels moved smoothly and the grade flattened into a ribbon of road as they traveled it, so that, while it was uphill work for the Parrish family, they finally reached the end at six o'clock on Sunday evening.

"It wasn't so bad," Penny said to her father as they watched Louise, her aunt and her luggage, rolling out the drive. "We walked to Fort Putt and she was a pretty good sport, even when she turned her ankle. Of course, she ditched Dick once to go into the Boodlers' with a second classman, but Dick didn't care. It would be funny if she'd really reformed, wouldn't it?"

"It would be fine," Major Parrish answered. "You kids can do a lot to help her."

"I know it." Penny's voice lost its enthusiasm. "But I hope we won't have to do it very soon."

"You probably won't. She'll be in school, now."

"And so will I. Isn't it awful, Daddy," she groaned, "that people have to be educated? Didn't you hate it?"

"I?" Her father looked down at her in shocked surprise. "Why, my dear daughter, I stood first in my class here at the Point."

"You did not!" Penny laughed and tucked her arm through his. "I've heard your classmates tease you. And don't forget that Mummy always tells how you were so scared you wouldn't stand high enough to make the cavalry that you broke dates with her to study—and she almost broke her engagement to you."

"You know too much, Miss Parrish," her father retorted. "But since you do, suppose you try to redeem the family honor as a student."

"All right, I'll try, but . . ."

"I've been thinking." Her father studied the shrubbery that garnished the front steps. "I've been thinking that perhaps we should become a two-car family. A small coupe might . . ."

"Oh, Daddy!" Penny clutched the lapels of his sport coat and spun him around to face her. "Do you mean we'll get another car? Really?"

"Well—it's four miles to your school. And you have to get

back and forth every day. Now, how the dickens are you going to do it?"

"Oh, my soul!" Her encircling arms were a vise around his neck. "You're the most wonderful father in the world."

"Keep calm, dear. It won't be a super de luxe car like Carrol's. It may even be second-hand."

"I don't care! I don't care what it is—if only it has four wheels and a motor inside it. Can't you just *see* me? I'll drive along and bow to people . . ." Penny closed her eyes in dreamy contemplation of her importance, then met her father's amused stare with a flush. "I do get so carried away," she explained. "But I'll be careful not to be selfish and monopolize the car all the time. Mummy will have to have it some, too. But I can be responsible for its gas and things, can't I?"

She looked at him so earnestly that he hugged her. "You can be responsible for all of it," he promised. "In fact, although everything the Parrish family has is on an equal sharing basis, we'll appoint you manager."

"David should be that," Penny answered thoughtfully. "But since he can't, I'll make a good one. And I'll ride him back and forth whenever he wants to come over home."

Her excitement was so great that, pulling her father with her, she raced inside to impart the news to Carrol. The buying of the car, which turned out to be a slightly used demonstrator of the latest model, was the biggest moment in her life. And even school seemed so enticing that she was ready every morning, a half hour ahead of time. With a condescending pat for the dazzled Bobby and Tippy, and a farewell kiss for her parents, she would sweep through the dining room in dramatic farewell. For a few mornings an armful of school books marred her exit, so she deposited them at the side door which opened into the garage, before she made her adieus. A dust cloth flipped across a shining green hood, and she was ready to take her place on her throne.

The thrill of her twenty minute trip back and forth to Briar-cliff carried her through the days, and at the end of the first month her report card overwhelmed her parents. Carrol and her father had moved into New York, and so it was only on week-ends that Penny could admire the two coupes, standing side by side.

So October hurried by and November stripped the leaves from the trees. Everyone talked football. Everyone searched the skies for clouds on Saturday, and cheered or groaned for the team. Of all the thousands who had tickets to see the Army gray meet the gold and blue of Notre Dame, in New York, no one was more excited than Penny. She and Carrol made their plans at night, in lengthy telephone conversations, and she reported faithfully on the exact schedule of the corps.

"They'll get in about eleven o'clock," she said in her final bulletin. "And Daddy says that he told your father *definitely* that our whole family will come late Friday afternoon—that's tomorrow. And Mummy wants to know, shall we bring Trudy to take care of the kids? Trudy's so scared of New York."

On being assured that Trudy was unnecessary, she shook her head at her mother and returned to her own and more important matters. "We can get up early and go to meet the ferry—the train dumps the corps over on the New Jersey side of the Hudson—and what do you think you'll wear?"

The resultant description caused so much anguish over her wardrobe that her father laughed and her mother sighed.

"I'll really have to get the child some clothes while I have her down there," Mrs. Parrish said, as Penny modeled her different outfits for their selection. "You wouldn't think she'd still be growing at fifteen."

She shook her head at the wrists that dangled from jacket sleeves, and did her best with hems and waistlines. Penny chose and discarded, packed and repacked, until, when she snapped the locks of her case, she was unable to remember what her final decisions had been.

"It will be a grand surprise of unmatched nothing," she said as she stowed her collection in the luggage compartment of the larger car. "I'll bet I haven't a single thing I'll want. Is Woofy going?"

"Of course not." Mrs. Parrish pulled Woofy from the back seat and passed him to Bobby. "Chuck him in the house," she commanded.

Bobby departed with a bundle of whines and howls, and the rest of the family settled themselves into their accustomed places.

"Seems funny not to be goin', too," Trudy said as she gave Tippy her favorite doll, Georgia. "Don't you forget to take good care of my child'n, and watch 'em when you're crossin' the streets."

"Oh, we will," Mrs. Parrish answered her meekly and peered past her for the missing Bobby. "We're getting off in the usual Parrish style," she commented. "Wouldn't you think that just *once* we could get into a car, sit down and *go?*"

"We did—once," her husband reminded her. "The time we took the Houghtons and David to the airport. Penny, go and find Bobby."

"I'll get him." Trudy departed, was lost herself, and finally returned with Bobby clutched firmly to her. "He was aputtin' on his cowboy suit," she said as she dumped him into the car and pushed a package after him. "I had to tell him he could take it with him."

She waved to them from the doorway as Major Parrish backed the car along the driveway. After three false starts, with return trips for forgotten articles, they were off. Penny sighed in relief when they breezed past the guard at the gates of the Post, then closed her mind to everything but the adventures that were to come.

The Houghton penthouse was as impressive as Gladstone Farms. After the elevator had whisked them up twenty-eight stories, it opened its doors into a vast apartment that had three more floors of its own, wide terraces, and a breath-taking view of the tallest city in the world.

"I feel awfully little, even way up here," Penny told Langdon Houghton as she stood on the wind-swept terrace, looking down on Central Park. "It's—it's all so big."

"It is big, Penny," he answered her. "And we are quite little people when we get down into it. But each one of us is important. Without us, it couldn't be so big."

"I know it. It seems strange that everyone down there has a life of his own, just like we have. I wish they could all be as happy as we are." She looked down on the moving dots and sighed. "People worry me," she concluded. "So many of them aren't happy."

"But we are, eh, Pen?" Mr. Houghton saw the troubled look on her face and hoped to erase it. "We're going to the football game."

"Umhum, we are." With that thought the joy in her own busy little life returned, and she rushed indoors to find Carrol.

The evening went by like a dream. When Carrol told her that two girls, classmates, were coming to dinner and would go to the theatre with them, she bustled about among her clothes and waited anxiously for Carrol's approval of her choice.

"Are the girls fun?" she asked as she took her place at the mirror.

"They're the ones I wrote you about—very upper-crust, and very boring. You know," Carrol's eyes met Penny's in the mirror, "I'm anxious to see how you make out with them. You're the only thing I've been able to talk about, so far, that interests them."

"Do they think I'm a cowgirl, or something?"

"No, but they think you're a sort of cross between Alice in Wonderland and a wild man in a circus."

Penny threw back her head and laughed. "I hope I won't let them down," she said.

But when she saw the girls, as they sat in the library looking at each other, there seemed to be no danger of letting them down—and no hope of buoying them up. Two more silent and conservative young ladies had never fallen to Penny's lot to entertain. Faith Carmichael was blond and insipid; Denise Dane, for all her chaste and expensive clothes, was definitely a mouse; a spoiled, petted mouse that ate only imported cheese.

"This," Carrol whispered as they went in to dinner, "is what you save me from, on week-ends. I showed you these two because they seem to be the best of the bunch."

"You're in the wrong school, darling," Penny answered. "There must be some good kids in New York. I'll have to get out and find them for you."

She slid into her place at Langdon Houghton's left and exchanged a merry wink with him.

"You have work cut out for you, just to your liking," he said. "How are you getting on?"

"I'm terriffic." Penny hunched her shoulders and bent toward him. "Louise seems such a simple problem, compared to these girls," she whispered. "But we'll manage them. Carrol and I are pretty good at problems." She turned to the girl beside her, Denise, the very mousy one, and was surprised to find her regarding Bobby and Tippy with displeasure.

"Don't they eat in the nursery?" Denise asked. "I didn't know small children ever come to the table."

"Ours do." Penny opened her napkin and laid it carefully across her lap. "You see, our children are part of our family, and we enjoy them quite a lot. Of course," she explained, "they don't have dinner with us when we have parties; but they belong to Carrol and her father, too. We're a family—and this isn't a party."

"Oh."

Denise devoted herself to her dinner as though she preferred to eat alone, and Penny listened to a long and toneless recital from Faith about her trip around the world. When it was time for the theatre, Penny and Carrol skipped into the elevator with last minute sallies for their elders, with Penny bouncing out again for her forgotten purse. The other two waited quietly, as completely passive as sheep; and as completely covered—if not with fleece—with fine, expensive fur. They were so richly wrapped that climbing into the long limousine behind them, Penny gave the wolf collar of her sport coat a loving little pat.

They drove through the park, and she and Carrol tossed a little ball of conversation back and forth like a game of catch. Between them, two sphinx-like faces turned from side to side, as obedient as a well-trained audience, with only smiles to approve their skill. They made no effort to join the game, but on Broadway, which the car traversed twice because Penny became ecstatic over the lights and signs, the haughty one sat up straighter to follow Penny's pointing finger, and the mouse made a remark that held the merest trace of wit.

"Nice going," Carrol whispered as they alighted at the theatre. "You're pepping them up." She turned to give the chauffeur his directions and smiled as Penny, rural, unsophisticated Penny, herded her two lambs into the lobby like a watchful shepherdess.

It was Penny, who, studying her programme, knew the history of the actors; who recognized the famous motion picture stars among the audience; who could discuss the plot of the play. She chatted in a soft excitement that kept the others bent toward her until the lights dimmed—then she left them as completely as though she had left a vacant chair.

Her eyes were on the stage and her hands were tense in her lap; but she, herself, was behind the footlights, talking and living with the actors in the world of make-believe.

When the curtain fell on a finished act, she sighed and shook herself, and although she answered the questions that were asked her, her replies were vague.

"I'll be an actress, someday," she told Carrol as they eased their way up the aisle after the last curtain call. "I know I could do that young girl's part." She slid her gloves onto fingers that still stung from applause and, as they waited for the car amid the jostle of the outpouring crowd, surveyed one brown suede hand critically. "A wedding ring will only lead to dishwater," she quoted, as though she were quite alone. "And I will never let you put one on my finger—not if I have to spend my life in gloves."

"That won't help you, dear," a voice beside her answered. "The only safeguard for you, is mittens."

Penny whirled. "Why—what . . ." Her face encountered that of Denise who had leaned over her shoulder; and Denise's little mouse teeth were showing in a smile.

"You said Kitty's lines from the play, so I answered you with Teddy's—I thought his were cuter than hers." Denise spoke in timid apology which was completely lost on Penny.

"Do you like to act?" Penny's voice held a new respect and she waited eagerly for an answer.

"I love to. We put on plays at school and . . ."

The car door was open and Penny stuffed Denise in ahead of her. "S'cuse me," she said to Carrol as she crawled across her. "I have to sit beside Denise; she likes to act."

"I do, too." Faith's contribution which she hoped would prove a passport into the inner circle was lost until Carrol leaned toward her.

"She'll get back to us, after a while," Carrol whispered. "Right now, she wouldn't hear it if the subway blew up."

"I can't believe it," Penny was repeating. "You certainly

don't *look* like an actress. But the way you *said* those *lines!* My goodness, I can't believe it."

"I know it." Denise's small face glowed. "I wish we could read some plays together."

"I do, too. Let's do it. How about tomorrow?"

"Why, Pen!" Carrol leaned across the row to look at Penny. "Tomorrow is the football game."

"Oh, so it is." Penny weighed the thrill of the football game against the advancement of her chosen career, and effected a compromise. "How about in the morning?" she suggested.

"The corps gets in in the morning. Don't you want to see that?"

"Well, yes I do. But my goodness, Carrol," her indecision was great. "I can see the corps any old time, and I can't get hold of Denise."

"Of course you can. You can come down on Fridays. And besides, Faith has been trying to tell you that she likes to act, too." Carrol began leading her deftly away from the precipice of her own enthusiasm. "I think we can all see a lot of plays, and then later on, try to do something on our own."

"I suppose you're right." Penny sighed and stared out into the dark. "I'm just so full of it right now that . . ."

"You always are, darling." Carrol laughed and shook her head. "The thing you're doing at the moment is the only thing you want to do. You know how David teases you about it."

"Yes. Well, . . ." Penny turned to the others and made a face. "Carrol's right. She usually is, and I suppose I'd feel awful if I missed the game. I'm kind of excited about that, too, but . . ." she looked at the two who had been boring acquaintances fifteen minutes ago, and felt that her life was hanging upon their decision . . . "would you come up to West Point for a week-end? Mummy could write to your mothers."

They assured her that they would enjoy nothing more;

and although their laborate acceptances might have been augmented by the thought of brass buttons and marching cadets, Penny had no such idea in mind. She had already set the sun room as a stage, and was seeing herself sweeping back and forth in flowing robes, while the others attended competently to less important roles. She told them good night in a flurry of plans, and stepped from the elevator into the Houghton apartment in a daze.

"I think I'll write a play," she told Carrol as they rifled the refrigerator. "I can make the parts fit better that way."

"Oh, Penny," Carrol sat on the kitchen table and waved the drumstick she was nibbling, "you simply slay me! You see *one* play—and then you not only become a famous actress in half an hour—but you write your way to stardom."

"I guess I am crazy." Penny laughed at herself as she sank gracefully down on the linoleum. "But after all, I'm fifteen years old. I haven't got much time to become famous in." She looked at her crossed ankles and at the hand that rested among the folds of her skirt. It's a nice pose, she thought, as she leaned her head against the white porcelain of the refrigerator. I must remember it so that I can use it in a play sometime.

★

CHAPTER V

A LOST PENNY

Carrol sat up in bed to look at the gray morning light that was filtering through the window pane.

It's going to be a dull, horrid day, she thought as she squinted at the bedside clock. Eight o'clock, and gloomy. Oh, dear. She looked across at the other twin bed, at the still-slumbering Penny, and fumbled for her slippers and robe.

" 'Morning, Daddy," she said as she came into the upstairs sitting room where her father was enjoying his breakfast and his newspaper. "Do you suppose it's going to snow, or something?"

"I don't believe so, dear. Let's see what the weather man has to say."

Together they searched the paper, and Carrol was relieved when they found a prediction of afternoon sunshine.

"Are you and Penny going to meet the corps?"

"I don't think so. Penny has to go shopping with her mother, so I thought I'd just wait until later, and then meet David at the Aldon Hotel—that's corps headquarters, you know. Are you and Major Parrish coming to lunch with us?"

Her father's eyes twinkled as he looked at her over his newspaper. "Don't you think we might be a little de trop?" he asked. "We haven't any brass buttons, and it's been a good many years since we were in college."

"You're always young." Carrol threw her arms around his neck and rested her chin on the top of his thick, dark hair.

48

"You're the youngest older people I have ever seen. I think the boys might be jealous of you."

He reached up to her and drew her around to his chair-arm as the Parrish family descended upon them with joyous good mornings and plans for the day. Marjorie Parrish struggled with what she hoped would be a time-saving list of stores and purchases, and Penny wandered around, still in a dramatic daze.

"You know," she said, as she zipped Tippy into her ski suit for a trip to the park, "when I'm an old lady I'll look back on this time as one of the brightest spots in my life. I'll say to my grandchildren, 'darlings, Grandmother would never have become a famous actress if she hadn't gone to visit at your Aunt Carrol's.'"

She smiled so tenderly at Tippy, that Bobby, stamping his feet into his galoshes, said, "Oh, nuts!" and Carrol laughed.

"What's an actress?" Tippy piped. "Is it what I was when I pretended to be Mrs. Santa Claus, in kindergarten?"

"Yes, darling." Penny arranged Tippy's curls under her blue cap. "Acting is a very old and noble profession."

A snicker from Carrol brought her head up, and she grinned and gave Tippy a push. "Scat," she ordered in her every-day voice. "I have to get ready to go to town."

She flew about the apartment, dressed and re-dressed until her mother was exasperated. "Penny, darling, please come down to earth," she begged. "We have to get off or I can't get you to the Aldon by twelve o'clock."

"Yas'm," Penny answered, in imitation of Trudy. "I sho' am in a tizzy this mornin'; but I'm ready."

"Have you that identification card I gave you, in case you get lost from me? And have you any money?"

"Nope, to both—at least I think so." Penny trotted back upstairs, searched through a bulging purse, and sat down at the desk to cover a sheet of notepaper with all the information about herself she could remember. She hastily scanned

the directory for the Houghton telephone number, then took
the stairs two at a time.

"Many, many thanks," she exclaimed, waving the five-dol-
lar bill her mother handed her. "Look, Carrol, I'm as rich as
a cream puff." She kissed the remaining spectators extrava-
gantly and skipped after her mother into the elevator. "I'll
bet you won't know me when you see me," she called back.
"But wait for me at the Aldon. You can tell me by my sweet,
smiling face."

The elevator whisked them down, leaving the apartment
very quiet. Carrol dressed leisurely, studying herself critically
in the mirror as she adjusted a bit of gray fur and ribbon that
was meant to be a hat. She was unconscious of her beauty as
she smoothed her shining blond curls, for she was wondering
if David were as excited about today as she was. She slipped
into her squirrel coat, looked again at her reflected self, then
impulsively went to kneel at a low bookcase in her sitting
room. From behind the books she lifted out a small box and
slipped off the lid. Two little twigs lay inside, coddled on a
bed of cotton, and she touched them gently.

"This is the day we planned, David," she whispered to the
longer twig as she held it up, "last summer on the night of
the moonlight picnic. You said you were the tall twig, and
I was the little twig—and now, here we are in New York,
just as you said we'd be. Oh, I hope it will be a perfect day!"

She put the box back in its resting place, fastened her soft,
gray coat at the throat, and went quietly down the stairs.

As she came into the Aldon Hotel, the lobby was crowded.
The corps was in. Gray overcoats were paired with fur coats;
smooth-cropped heads bent toward curls of every color; and
bass and treble mingled in a hum. Carrol wove her way in
and out among the crowd; smiled a greeting to some, and
was followed by an admiring stare from many others. David
was standing by a pillar and his eyes lighted up when he saw
her.

"Hello, little twig," he said as he came to meet her. "Here we are."

"Hello, David. Isn't it thrilling?"

Their hands clasped and David drew her back to his pillar. "There isn't a spot to sit down," he pointed out, "but we can lean here for a bit and then go somewhere and have a coke. I told Dick and Michael we'd meet 'em here."

"Penny's apt to be late, because she's gone shopping with your mother."

"Oh, heck! Then there's no telling when she'll turn up. I went shopping with Mums, once."

They shouted to each other, and side-stepped as people, young and old and talking victory, squeezed by them; until at last, David said: "Let's go in the florist shop and get your chrysanthemum. I thought we'd wait until Penny got here, but you look so undecorated."

"All right." She nodded to him, followed through the way he opened up for her, and watched his long, clever fingers pinning the yellow flower, with its bow of gold and gray and black, to her coat.

When he had it securely fastened, he smiled down at her and said, "Pretty nice day, isn't it?"

"It's a wonderful day." Carrol knew how much the few simple words meant when they came from David, so she said again: "It's the most wonderful day I've ever known. Oh, David, isn't it *fun?*"

"You bet it is. And it's all I can do to keep from jumping around like Penny or yelling like Bobby. I'm trying so darned hard to be dignified."

He paid for the flower and they fought their way through the mob again to their post. Louise went by, flanked by two cadets, and the wave she sent them was airy. Dick and Michael loomed up, caps in hand, the capes of their overcoats folded back in two neat triangles.

"This is stuffy," Dick complained as they tried to talk above the noise. "I feel like a monkey in the zoo. Let's get out."

"Okay." David and Carrol followed them, and outside Michael asked,

"Where's Penny?"

"Gone to get herself dressed up for the occasion." David was glum in his explanation. "I don't see why Mums always chooses a time like this to shop. We'll be late for lunch, and the corps has to form at one o'clock. Have you got your ticket, Carrol?"

"Yes, Penny brought it to me."

"I wish we could sit with you; but I know where I got your seat, and I'll meet you between halves. Gosh, I wish Penny would come along."

Penny was coming along—just as fast as a fascinating selection of ensembles would let her. At last she saw herself in a wine-colored three-piece suit; the fronts of the top coat banded with lynx, and the shoulders squarely padded.

"My goodness, I never had so much fur on me!" she exclaimed softly as she stroked her chest. "And I've even got a little fur halo around my neck."

The saleswoman turned away her head to smile before she set a wine and fur concoction on Penny's head. New gloves and a purse were brought, and Penny, although briefly dazzled by her glory, snatched them up and flung her arms around her mother.

"I'm so happy," she whispered. "But don't you think it's too expensive? I'd like the cheaper suit all right."

"It *is* expensive." Her mother hugged her tightly as she answered. "But this is the suit I want you to have; and it's less than I thought we'd have to pay, so run along and enjoy yourself." She watched Penny take one last whirl before the mirror and added, "Have you changed the contents of your old purse to the new?"

"I'll do it, pronto." Penny began dumping the odds and

ends from one bag to the other as she answered. "Even my lost-and-found directions and my money and my ticket. I'm all set, and I'll take a cab to the Aldon."

I wonder if I should have gone with her? her mother thought as she saw Penny off, and stood looking after the taxi. "She's so scatter-brained."

Penny rolling along, listening to the radio and admiring herself, felt anything but scatterbrained. She paid her driver with great care, counted her change and gave him his tip; then, feeling very important, she walked up the hotel steps. In the lobby, which had begun to thin, she glanced about for her own little crowd. There was no sign of them, so she stood by the cigar counter, waiting patiently. Girls and boys were hurrying in and out, and a worried frown was creasing her brow when she spied Louise.

"Have you seen Carrol or David or Mike?" she asked, catching Louise by the sleeve.

"Oh, hello; no I haven't—not since I first came. They were here, and then they all went out together. Have you lost them?"

"Not exactly, but . . ." Penny sighed and clutched her new purse tighter. "I'm kind of late, I guess. They've probably gone out for some lunch. If you see them, will you tell them that I got safely back?"

"All right." Louise took a step forward, then turned back to Penny. "Have you got your ticket?" she asked.

"Umhum, I have it—so I'll be all right. See you at the game."

" 'By." Louise went on and Penny, shifting from one foot to another, felt an aching desire for food. She opened her purse, saw that her ticket was there, her money was there, then made a dash for the connecting drug store. A group of girls called to her but she only stopped for a brief hello, before she dashed out and down the steps.

Doors so often play an important part in peoples' lives.

One can walk through a door to adventure; one can fail to find a door, and so miss a golden opportunity; or one can do as Penny did—walk in a door, just as one's friends walk out another.

Carrol and her three companions, unconscious of Penny's proximity, returned to the hotel lobby and their waiting. Louise, still there, hurried to them. Her eyes lighted on Dick and Michael and, unattended now, she hoped to have companionship to the stadium.

"Hi," she called. "Can't you find Penny?"

"No. Have you seen her?" Carrol was worried. Worried for Penny's safety, and worried because the boys must leave quickly if they were to fall into their places in the corps, for its triumphal march onto the football field.

"She was here, but she left. She said she was late and supposed you had gone on to lunch."

"Did she say that she'd come back?" Michael was holding a tempting yellow chrysanthemum, and Louise coveted it as she answered lightly:

"No. She said she had her ticket—and then she went out. She said she'd see me at the game."

"Well, Pen can take care of herself, but I don't understand it." David looked at Louise closely. "Are you sure she said she'd go on?" he asked.

"Well, David, that's what I understood. But I saw her speak to Mary Jane McGuire over there. You can ask her."

David walked across to the group of girls Louise pointed out, talked for a few moments, and returned. "They don't know a thing," he said. "She just said hello and went on. We've got to get out to the stadium in nothing flat."

"I'll wait here," Carrol suggested. "She might come back."

"She won't." Louise was positive. "You know Pen. She makes up her mind and away she goes."

"Yeah." David looked around the now empty lobby. "We may as well all go," he decided. "She knows what subway to take, and she'll be sitting in her seat, full of excuses, by the time we get there."

"Lead on." Michael handed his chrysanthemum to Carrol with a "keep this for her" and they hurried out. Louise, without explanation, joined them, and her eyes were on the extra flower.

"My drag went on before I was ready," she said as they squeezed into the crowded train. "I hope you don't mind my tagging."

"We're glad to have you." Carrol clung to a strap, swaying with the car. When a curve threw her against David, she whispered: "I do hope Penny's there."

But Penny wasn't there. Her seat was empty, and it stayed empty as the minutes ticked away. Carrol's glove was off that she might see her watch, and she said repeatedly to the girls around her, "Oh, I do want her to see the corps come in— she's looked forward to it so."

She stood up, scanned the crowd and sat down again; stood up and sat down. The band began to play and the long lines of gray marched out onto the field. A lump came into her throat as, instead of watching the marching Army, she was straining to find Major and Mrs. Parrish among the standing spectators.

Where is *Daddy?* she thought frantically. He'd know what to do. But three people among fifty thousand are difficult to find, and even a trip around the outside aisle failed to help her. The corps broke ranks to find their seats; a whistle blew —and the game was on.

Up and down the field went the ball, and around and around the stadium went Carrol's eyes. Even David was lost in the gray blur that filled the next section; and the minutes that held others spellbound were only torture to her. When the whistle blew for the end of the half, she was out of her seat and away.

"David!" she cried as they met at the arranged exit. "She hasn't come!"

"Good grief!" David took off his cap and turned it help-lessly in his hands. "I don't know what to do, Carrol. It's no good going back to the Aldon, even if I dared leave, for she isn't there now. Perhaps she couldn't find the way and has gone home."

"I'll go somewhere and telephone as soon as the crowd sits down."

"It won't do any good, honey. And don't cry." David put his arm around her shoulders. "If she's there—she's there. You couldn't get her out here in time to see any of the game. And nothing's going to happen to Penny; it never does. Maybe she and Mums went shopping again. Louise is so half-baked she wouldn't know what Pen said."

"Yes, and maybe Louise just made us come on so that she could come out with Michael. She does things like that, and we shouldn't have trusted her."

"I thought of that. That's why I talked to those other girls. I guess she was honest this time. No, I think Penny went back to Mums."

"Do you really?"

"Yes. Let's have a hamburger."

Carrol became conscious of the curious stares their little conference was receiving. For while David was unaware that his comforting arm still lay about her shoulders, their pose and her tears suggested a lover's quarrel to outsiders; and she flushed and drew away. "All right," she nodded.

" 'Atta girl." David gave her the handkerchief he carried in his cap, still unconcerned for the cadets and girls who were crowding past him, and went on to say, "I know you're wor-ried, and I could murder Pen for spoiling your day. But she's all right—she always is. So, smile."

He looked down at her as he linked his arm through hers, and her troubled eyes came up to meet his calm, steady gaze. "You're always such a help, David."

"Well, it's such a pleasure to help you. It's no trouble at all. Now, on to the hamburger stand."

All through the next quarter, Carrol searched the sea of faces. When the goals were changed for the final period, she could stand it no longer, so crawled past the row of shouting maniacs into the aisle. Marjorie Parrish had worn a black felt in the morning, but the bright face under a red turban that finally caught Carrol's eye was only identified in the last few minutes of the game. She waited until a final groan from the corps told the sad tale for Army, then pushed her way through the crowd that surged toward her.

"Mrs. Parrish! Major Parrish!" she called, struggling to reach them. "Penny hasn't come to the game!"

"Good heavens!" Major Parrish was beside her and the joyous face under the red turban was suddenly pale.

"Oh, Carrol, are you *sure?* Where *is* she? Oh, I *knew* I shouldn't have let her . . ."

"Now, Marjorie, keep calm." Major Parrish stopped the torrent of words. "You always get so excited—and Penny is probably at home having a fit because she missed the game. We'll go and telephone, dear, and then we'll find Lang and the car." He took charge of the situation, then turned to Carrol. "Keep my fuss-budget with you," he directed. "Collect David, and meet your father at D gate. I'll telephone, and then pick you up—all fears allayed. Is that clear?"

"I understand. Come on, Mrs. Parrish." Carrol, her heart leaden, looked at the trembling lips under the gay red hat, and tried to pretend a confidence she was far from feeling. "Everything will be all right."

Together, they found David, and his terse, "Quit worrying, Mums. You know Pen's all right," did much to restore his mother's hopes while they searched for D gate and Langdon Houghton. But when she saw the serious face of her husband approaching, saw him shake his head and say a few words to David who had gone to meet him, her fears possessed her again.

"Oh please, let's hurry," she begged. "Let's go *somewhere!*"

"We're going, dear."

The car drew up and she was inside before the chauffeur could spring down to open the door. "Where shall we go?" she asked. "Where can one *look* in New York?"

"Home, first." Langdon Houghton got in beside her and laid the robe across her knees. "Don't be frightened, Marjorie. We must keep our heads in this thing and try to figure out what Penny would do if she were left behind. I don't think she'd go home and just sit, do you?"

"No."

"Then, she's probably at a movie. If Penny can't do one thing, you know she'll do something else." He leaned forward and spoke to the chauffeur. "We'll go home, Parker," he ordered.

"Yes, sir."

Parker drove as rapidly as he could, watching the traffic lights and easing the car in and out through the crowded streets. He liked the voluble Penny, who always found time to talk with him about his little boy's infantile paralysis and to send him cut-out books and toys. So he waited at the curb after the family had disappeared indoors, and shook his head sadly when word was brought down that he was to eat his dinner quickly and have the car in readiness for any emergency.

The hours dragged by. Six o'clock. Seven. Eight.

"I don't know what to do now," Major Parrish said with a sigh when he returned from a fruitless search of all the hospitals. "The servants have a list of the telephone calls,—there were only three—and Lang has the police on the watch."

"There isn't anything to do—but wait." Marjorie Parrish pushed aside a small table that held her untasted dinner. "I think . . ." she looked at David, then at Michael who had slipped quietly in . . . "I think if you could all eat something it would be better for you. Penny isn't hurt, we know that much now—and when she comes . . ."

"She *is* coming, soon, Mrs. Parrish, dear." Carrol bent to lay her cheek against the chestnut waves that were so like Penny's. "Wouldn't you like another cup of coffee?"

"Thank you, dear, I'd love to have one." Mrs. Parrish drew Carrol down to her and said with a smile, the first she had dared since she came into the house: "And please say Aunt Marjorie. I think we should all be uncles and aunts to each other, don't you? I've meant to suggest it for some time."

"I think it would be practically . . ." Carrol thought of Penny as she used her favorite word, broke off with a gulp and said instead: "I'll get your coffee, Aunt Marjorie."

David found her in the pantry, her hands searching blindly along the shelf for a cup.

"Carrol, honey."

The tears spilled over. "I can't bear it," she sobbed. "We went off and left Penny—and your mother's so sweet and frightened and. . . . Oh, David, what if something *terrible* has happened!"

David opened his arms to her, and her bright head was crushed against him.

The clock struck nine. And still no Penny.

★

Court Martial

"Thank you dear, for the coffee." Mrs. Parrish took a sip from the steaming cup, then listened to the whir of the approaching elevator.

So many times during the dragging hours it had come up —with all eyes focused on the mahogany doors. So many times they had opened, with only a weary searcher emerging; and so many times the hum of the approaching car had brought the watchers to attention, only to retreat from a lower floor, and to drop them back again. Now it came on and on. The group in the drawing-room peered into the foyer, watching, listening, and erect in their chairs.

Who can it be? Langdon Houghton thought with a shudder. We're all here now. If it's the police. . . .

There was a soft click. The car stopped, and the doors slid open.

"Yoohoo, everybody. I'm practically . . ." Penny dashed out,—saw the roomful of staring faces, and stopped. "Why, what's the matter?" she asked blankly.

"Oh, *Penny!*" Her mother flew across the carpet. "We've been so frightened. Where were you?"

"Why," Penny disentangled herself from the smothering embraces and dabbed at her face that was covered with her mother's tears. "Didn't you know?"

"Of course, we didn't know." Her father, reacting from his fright became stern. "How *could* we know?"

"But . . . Well. . . ." Penny looked at them all, pressed so close to her, and her dazed mind refused to grasp the shock her return had been to them. "My goodness, Mike," she said, "I forgot all about you. I'm awfully sorry."

"Well, sorry—nothing! Where've you been? And what have you been doing?" David crowded in closer and broke the spell.

"Why, I. . . . My goodness, didn't you get my messages?"

"We didn't get any messages, Penny." Mr. Houghton took her coat from her unprotesting arms and led her to a chair. "Suppose you sit down and tell us all about it."

"Well," Penny sat down, only to rush to her mother and father again. "Oh, darlings, I'm so sorry," she cried as alternately she covered their faces with kisses. "I didn't dream that you wouldn't know. I *did* telephone."

"It's all right now—so sit down and end our suspense." Her father gave her a pat and she went back to her seat, the sparkle leaping into her eyes again. "It was marvelous!" she said rapturously. "I can't believe that anything like it could happen to me! But I want you to know, I did telephone."

"Okay. So you telephoned. Go on." David, on an ottoman before her, prodded her relentlessly.

"Well, after I met Miss Ware I rushed to a . . ."

"After you met whom?"

"Miss Ware. You see, the car skidded . . ."

"What car?"

"The car that didn't stop for the light. Oh, dear, you get me so mixed up." Penny glared at David. "If I could just begin at the beginning and tell it my way . . ."

"Go on, Penny, for heaven's sake, tell it your way. It's the only way you'll tell it in the end, so we might as well be comfortable." Her father nodded his approval, drew his limp wife to the divan with him, and motioned to the others. When they were seated in a group around her, Penny launched forth.

"Well, of course you know that I missed Carrol and David and Mike. How did I ever happen to do that?" she asked.

"I wouldn't know. But if it could be done, you'd do it." David leaned toward her. "Where were you at game time?"

"I was in the drug store. I felt hungry and thought I'd dash in and catch a malted milk because Louise had said . . ."

"Oh! *Louise* had said!" David looked at the two who had encountered Louise with him and they all nodded solemnly. "Go on."

"Well, the place was crowded and I guess it took longer than I thought it would. So when I came back you must have gone on. I waited around a while; but there wasn't anyone there but a lot of bellhops with dust pans, so I decided to go to the game by myself. I still have my ticket," she added proudly. "Can Michael get his money back?"

"No—but it doesn't matter. Carry on, Pen." Michael leaned forward and smiled.

"That's too bad. Anyhow—I came out of the hotel. I wasn't sure whether I should take a train marked E or one marked C, so I sort of stood on the corner trying to decide which way the subway was."

"In other words," her father's eyes held an irrepressible amusement, "you were somewhat lost."

"Yes, I was. Or I knew I would be if I didn't think about it. So I was thinking. Just then the light changed to red and a car that was going too fast screeched on its brakes and tried to stop. I looked up and saw an awfully pretty girl—I thought she was a young girl then, but she turned out to be a woman —well, she came dashing along, trying to get out of the way of the car, and when she got to the curb, right at my feet, mind you—she fell down.

"I helped pick her up and a crowd gathered as though it were a fire or something; and the policeman stopped everything and came right over. He said, 'Are you hurt, Miss

Ware?' And she said, 'No, I'm all right—but get this crowd away.' He did the best he could; and of course I couldn't go because she was holding onto me. I thought she looked familiar but I couldn't figure out who she could be. Then she asked me if I minded walking along with her."

"Penny, I've told you not to talk to strangers." Her mother frowned at her and Penny grinned.

"She wasn't a stranger. She knelt right down at my feet. And anyway, she's a friend now. Well, we hobbled along, and she said, 'It was stupid of me to get out of the taxi on the other side of the street. My theatre is right here.' So *then*, I knew who she was. She's Janice Ware."

Penny paused impressively and waited for some show of excitement, but only Carrol said, "Really, Pen? Go on."

"I took her to the stage door . . . Are you *sure* you know who she is?"

"We certainly do know. And we're very much impressed." Mr. Houghton nodded to her. "I've seen Janice Ware on the stage and in the movies many times. She's a very fine actress."

"Oh, she is! I saw her act this afternoon." Penny clasped her hands and closed her eyes. For a second she saw Janice Ware behind the footlights, then with a sigh she returned to her own audience. "She asked me if I would like to come in with her and see the play. Of course I wanted to, but I said that I'd have to telephone home and she said that I could do it in her dressingroom. Oh, Mummy," Penny drew in a long breath and closed her eyes again, "the theatre smelled marvelous. It was sort of dusky in there, and men were running around with furniture and people were talking. It was noisy; but it was sort of hushed, too, as though everyone were waiting for something wonderful to happen. Before I could see very much, we went down a corridor with lots of closed doors, and one door had a star painted on it. Miss Ware opened it, and there was the most beautiful room, with flowers and a maid and everything—just like I want to have." Her voice crescendoed with emotion, then dropped to a practicality. "She showed me the telephone and I called up."

"What did you say, Pen?"

"Well, Daddy, I was so excited that I just asked if Mr. Houghton was there. And when the man, I guess it was Perkins, said no, he'd gone out, I said to tell him that I was Penny Parrish and that I'd gone to the theatre instead of the football game, and that I'd come home afterward."

"I can't understand it." Mr. Houghton shook his head. "You said Houghton, and your name, so you must have had the right number—and yet the servants declare that you didn't call."

"But I did. And then I went in to see the play."

Again Penny withdrew from them into the make-believe world she had known that afternoon. She could hear Janice Ware's throaty voice carrying her to heights she had never dreamed she could reach. Every word, every gesture was food for her hungry little mind to feast on for months to come.

"And what did you do afterward? The show didn't last *this* late."

"What, Davy? Oh. Why, I went back to her dressing-room. She asked me to because she said that, on matinee days, she just goes across to Hardy's for her dinner, and that she'd like me to come, too. I *wanted* to go, but of course I thought about tonight and my date with Mike, and then I decided that I could eat quickly and get home in time. That's when I telephoned again. But this time a maid answered and said no one was there."

"But we *were* here," her father interrupted her. "Let's get this straight. What number did you call?"

"Why, I don't know—but it's right, because I looked it up this morning. It's in my purse."

David brought her purse to her and she fumbled about until she triumphantly produced the piece of notepaper. "Here it is. Whitehall 7-8062."

"Penny! That's Daddy's office phone!"

"It is?" Penny looked blankly at Carrol. "But I copied it out of the book. It was the only one in there."

"I know it is." Mr. Houghton turned to the Parrishes. "Our house phone is a private number that is only given to people by Carrol or me. Even our own servants don't know it because it isn't in the directory. But you have it, Penny; you've called Carrol."

"Only once." Penny was chagrined but determined to defend herself. "It's so expensive that Carrol always calls me. And besides, it's written on Mummy's desk pad."

"Of course. Then you got hold of my secretary the first time. Carson, being a little on the stupid side, would never think to relay the message to the house. The last call, I don't doubt, was taken by a scrub woman after office hours. Penny, you couldn't have messed it up better if you tried."

"I know it." Penny looked unhappy; then she grinned. "If it hadn't been that I met Miss Ware and a lot of movie stars I'd be simply sick about it."

"Did you really meet movie stars, Pen?"

"Yep, I did. We went into Hardy's, and the head waiter bowed almost double. He trotted along ahead of us to a table by the wall that Miss Ware always has, and everyone stared at us. You know," Penny looked eagerly at her mother, "it was such a comfort to me to know that I looked nice. Of course," she considered the matter carefully, "I might have had a good time in my old school coat because I'm not vain, but I don't believe Miss Ware would have been so keen to have me. It's funny about clothes, isn't it?"

"Yes, very funny." David could see her side-tracked like a cruising locomotive, so he threw the switch to the main line. "Go on."

"You hurry me so! Well, we sat down and the waiter gave

me a menu that was almost as big as I was. The prices were simply staggering and I didn't know what to do. I just looked up one side and down the other until Miss Ware finally took the menu and laid it on the table and laughed. Then she ordered us a perfectly marvelous dinner. We had onion soup and . . ."

"How did you meet the movie stars?"

"Oh, David," Penny scowled in annoyance. "You're so cut and dried about it."

"Well, you'd be cut and dried, too, if you'd been looking for somebody for nine hours and then all you got to hear was about what she ate. I'd like to get some dancing in tonight."

"I forgot about the dancing." Penny leaned over and caught his face between her hands. "My poor little pet," she said contritely, rubbing her nose against his, "You haven't had any fun at all. I'll hurry and tell the rest of it. Oh, Davy, I'm so selfish and so sorry." She slid off her chair to hug him and David sighed.

"Honestly, Pen, you're hopeless," he groaned. "Here you go on another tangent."

"Well, I am sorry." Penny forgot her new suit as she tried to share the ottoman with him. "And even if I did meet Jimmy Stewart . . ."

"Was he there, Pen?"

Carrol and Michael were down beside her, too, and her mother and father, with Mr. Houghton, were leaning forward.

"Umhum, he was having dinner with some people and he stopped and spoke to us. He was so friendly. And then, after he'd gone, Katharine Hepburn waved to us—oh, she's darling! But her hair sort of hung down like mine, and that made me feel better. And then Frank Morgan was there with some people, and Eddie Cantor. . . . Really, it was like a night in Hollywood."

She looked around so happily that her mother, dreading the reckoning that must come, sighed before she nudged her husband. Major Parrish cleared his throat twice before he could say quietly: "Come here, Penny."

She hopped up and ran to him and, as he held out his hand, settled herself on his lap. "Scoldings, in the Parrish family have never been very private affairs," he explained to the others. "We feel that a discussion of our mistakes will help the others not to make them, so we usually hold a general court martial."

"I know, Daddy. I shouldn't have gone. I was a sentry who deserted his post."

"No, you shouldn't have gone, Pen. You're an Army girl, and you know what it means to obey orders. Your orders were to report to the stadium. You failed in that. And you failed again when you weren't sure that your telephone communication reached headquarters. You've given us your side of the testimony, and you have had a wonderful experience; one that your mother and I are grateful you've had. But through your negligence, the rest of us have had a pretty tough time."

"I know it. Do you suppose I can ever make it up to you?"

"I imagine that you can. We'll probably hear enough about it in the next few weeks to feel that it happened to us. But these boys are like Pippa, in Browning's immortal poem; they have only one day to enjoy. You've cost them a good deal of it."

"I have, haven't I?"

"Yes. They want to go dancing—to say nothing of having some food."

"Haven't they eaten dinner?"

"They were much too upset, and much too busy trying to find you to think of eating either *lunch* or dinner."

"Oh, dear. I have been disloyal." Penny stood up and

looked from David to Michael. "They'd better go on, right away."

Her father looked at them, too, and his eyes were non-committal as he asked: "What are the findings of the court?"

"I find the prisoner guilty of neglect of duty, sir," David answered promptly.

"And I recommend the clemency of the court." Michael's voice hurried into the pause that followed David's words.

"And you, Marjorie?"

Mrs. Parrish's eyes were tender as they rested on Penny. "I'm awfully sorry to have to say it, dear," she answered in a whisper, "but I find you guilty, too."

"I know it." Penny glanced at Mr. Houghton, and then at Carrol whose heartache was in her eyes. "I guess you all feel the same way. It's like officers having to trust their soldiers. I usually think of that when Mummy and Daddy expect something of me, but somehow, today, I just didn't think at all." She turned to face her father. "Apologies aren't so hot," she said, "afterward, when it's too late. I've never had much sympathy for people who do that sort of thing, and then expect everything to be all right. But I'm really sorry, Daddy. I feel like a heel."

"I know you do, Pen." Her father held out his hand. "Come here a minute."

She went close to him, holding tightly to his big strong fingers as he spoke to her. "You've been found guilty because you are guilty. I can't grant the clemency that Michael requests, because misdemeanors must carry punishment. But I *can* suspend your sentence."

"You mean—that I could go dancing, too?"

"Yes, we could put it that way. It wouldn't be fair for your punishment to affect the others. Michael and David have been delayed enough as it is, and I imagine that Carrol wouldn't go without you." He pulled her to him and his lips were against her ear as he added: "Perhaps your mother will make the sentence very light. My culprit knew she was guilty and admitted it."

"Oh Daddy, you're a darling!" Penny kissed his cheeks and pulled her mother into her embrace. "I'll be so good that the sentence will stay suspended forever."

"I hope so." Major Parrish freed himself, pulled her to her feet and marched her across the room. "Here is your prisoner, boys," he said. "For heaven's sake, don't lose her."

CHAPTER VII

TOO MANY HEROINES

Penny sat at her window and contemplated the gray sky that wrapped itself around the sun like a soiled and ragged blanket. Now and then she sighed, shook herself and slumped lower in her chair. At last, with a resolute squaring of her shoulders, she got up and went into her mother's room.

"Mums," she said from the door, "I guess I'll have to talk to you. May I come in a minute?"

"Of course, darling." Mrs. Parrish looked up from her sewing with a smile. "Come in and sit down."

Penny crossed the room slowly, but instead of adopting her usual comfortable sprawl, stood with clenched hands resting on the back of a chair. "I've been thinking," she began, "that since you and Daddy haven't set any punishment for me—about that trouble I gave you in New York, I mean—perhaps *I'd* better do it. I know it's kind of queer for a criminal to sentence himself, but . . ." she concentrated on her fingers that were white as they pressed together, and hurried on. . . . "I tried to think of the thing that would be hardest for me to do—and then when I knew what it was, I tried to find something else. But I couldn't." Her breath caught as though trying to block the words that came tumbling out. "I guess I'll have to give up driving the little car."

"Oh, Penny." Her mother held tightly to her sewing, her hands yearning to smooth the troubled face before her. "Are you sure you want to give up the car? You're looking forward to the Christmas dance. Wouldn't that do just as well?"

"No. I thought about that, too. I do want to go to the dance, terribly. But the car's the most important thing to me of anything I have. That's what David would do if he had to decide, and it's what I have to do. I brought you the keys." She took the black leather case with its treasured driver's license from her pocket and laid it in her mother's hesitant fingers.

"But your school, Penny? We bought the car so you could get back and forth to school."

"I know it. But there's a bus that goes over that way about half-past six. I'll just have to get up and get on it."

Mrs. Parrish sighed. "I was afraid you would decide on something drastic," she lamented, "so I've been meaning to suggest the Christmas dance. I put it off because I couldn't bring myself to do even that. However, since you've made your offer, there's only one thing I can do. I'll have to accept it. How long a term do you think you should serve?"

"That's what I wondered about. Do you think it should be all winter?"

"Of course not, sweet. That would be a bit *too* extreme." Mrs. Parrish turned toward her desk and motioned Penny to bring her the small calendar that lay on it. "Let me see," she said as she looked at the dates. "How would Thanksgiving do, that's almost two weeks away?"

"Oh, Mummy," Penny hung over the calendar, her face clearing, "that's only twelve days. Do you think it *would* be enough?"

"It's really too long for comfort." Mrs. Parrish tossed her sewing away as Penny's arms closed around her. "I think you're a very sweet child," she said into the brown curls that covered her face, "and I think Daddy, and even David, will be satisfied."

"I hope so." Penny's head came up and she looked intently at her mother. "There's just one thing more. I thought about this, too. Do you think it would be fair for me to go on looking after the car? Buying its gas and oil, I mean?"

Her mother considered the matter gravely. "I don't believe it would," she decided. "If you're going to be heroic, you'd better go the whole way."

"That's what I thought. Only . . ." her eyes on her mother's upturned face were apologetic . . . "I hate to criticize you, darling, but you know you're kind of forgetful."

"Yes, I know I am."

"And you might neglect to have the battery filled."

"Umhum."

"And to check the air in the tires."

"I do, sometimes."

"So . . ." Penny spoke hesitantly . . . "perhaps I'd better make you a list. I'll fasten it on your mirror."

"That would help a lot. And of course you can remind me sometimes."

"Oh, I'll remind you every day."

Mrs. Parrish sighed as she looked at her enthusiastic sufferer. "Penny," she asked curiously, "do you enjoy being a heroine to yourself?"

"No." Penny shook her head but she answered cheerfully enough. "When you have something to do, you might as well do it. My conscience feels pleasantly satisfied, but I hope it gets as tired as the rest of me when we have to get up at half-past five." She walked across the room with a firm, light step, relieved that a difficult decision had been made, but her voice was unsteady as she turned in the door. "I put a clean dust cloth in the package compartment," she said. "You *will* dust every day, won't you?"

"I'll dust and dust." Her mother smiled and nodded, and Penny bolted for the stairs.

She was sitting in disconsolate state in the sunroom when Bobby and Tippy tracked her down. "Will you take us to the Post Exchange, Penny?" Bobby asked, climbing over the end of the divan. "We want to buy some candy."

"No, my little man." Penny gave him a gentle push and curled her feet under her. "I won't be chauffeuring anybody for quite some time."

"Why not?" Tippy edged her face under Penny's and looked up curiously.

"Because. . . ." Penny stared into space with wrinkled brows. "I wonder what Mums meant by saying that I'm being heroic?" she thought aloud. "It sounds kind of good."

She slid down into the pillows and Bobby pulled at her sweater sleeve. "What's heroic mean?" he questioned.

"It means doing something very brave. Like I'm doing."

"You aren't doing anything. You're just sitting. And that doesn't look very—very—heroic."

"Oh, but it is." Penny grinned at him, amused by his avid little mind that stored away knowledge for future use as a squirrel stores away nuts. "You see, I did something quite naughty," she explained patiently, "so, I gave up driving the car to atone for it. Now I just sit. Do you understand?"

"I guess so. But does just not driving the car make you heroic?"

"Yes. You see, I love to drive the car. But I won't drive it, so that is very heroic. And when I'm heroic that means I'm a heroine."

She watched him as he twisted and turned his information. His blue gaze blinked steadily at her, like an electric sign that goes on, then off, in perfect timing; and his face was as blank as the wall that holds it. After an interminable silence, he asked solemnly:

"Could I be a heroine?"

Penny shook her head. "Only girls are heroines," she told him.

"Oh." His gaze wavered to Tippy who was leaning against Penny, lost in a daydream of her own. "Could *she?*"

"She might, but I doubt it." Penny tweaked Tippy's curls. "She's never very naughty, you know."

"Nope. She isn't." Bobby sighed, then surveyed Tippy hopefully. "But she might be."

"She might; but I still doubt it. Now run along." Penny closed her eyes and, knowing that no more information would be forthcoming, Bobby took Tippy's small hand in his grubby paw. "Come on, Tip."

He regarded her speculatively as he led her out and, as a great idea was taking shape in his mind, urged quiet and caution when he crowded her into a secluded corner of the breakfast room.

"Listen," he whispered when the swinging door had squeaked to behind them. "How would you like to be a heroine?"

"I wouldn't like it," Tippy answered emphatically. "What is it?"

"Penny just told you. It's sumpin' nice. Everybody makes a fuss over you."

"How could I get to be one?" Tippy's doubt of him was vanishing in a desire for public approval, so she not only let him boost her onto a chair, but leaned toward him as he seated himself across the table.

"It's easy. You just do sumpin' kind of bad, then you do sumpin' kind of brave,—and you're a heroine."

"Hunhunh. You be it." Tippy began to slide from her chair but Bobby's arm forestalled her.

"Now wait a minute!" he urged. "I can't be it, 'cause after what Penny said, they'd all suspect me. Besides, only girls can be heroines. I'd be one if I could. I can't be one, so I'll help you."

"If I get spanked, will you get spanked, too?" Tippy's eyes were wide upon him, but she was weakening, so he nodded quickly.

"Sure. But heroines don't get spanked. They get ice cream and everybody kisses 'em."

"Oh." Ice cream, even in the dead of winter, had a magic sound, so Tippy threw caution to the winds. "What do I do?" she asked eagerly.

"Well, now I have to think." Bobby lapsed into study, elbows on the table, his chin in his hands. "You might talk back to Mummy," he suggested when Tippy had given up hope of becoming a heroine, at least during her childhood.

"Oh, I couldn't do that!" Not even ice cream was worth that price. Not even ice cream with chocolate sauce poured over it. "That's wicked, Bobby." She prepared to dismount again, and only Bobby's quick suggestion kept her fat legs from reaching the floor.

"I guess it doesn't have to be anything very much," he compromised. "It's really what you give up afterward that makes a heroine of you. You can just put some dirt in Trudy's milk and cream, or sumpin'."

"Would that be bad?"

"Naw, she can buy some more."

"All right." It seemed more trouble to mount the chair again than to slide on down and, as the idea was still vague, she trotted to the kitchen and stood before the refrigerator. "You'll have to hold me up."

"I can't do that." Bobby saw himself becoming an accomplice to her crime, so he put his hands behind him and stood like a small Satan urging an unsuspecting Eve. "But I could kind of give a chair a push."

"Okay." Tippy stopped the chair as it skidded past her, mounted and, with the caution of a burglar at a safe, began her looting. "I haven't any dirt," she grunted as she set the last bottle on the floor, "and it's awful cold outdoors. Could I pour it down the sink?"

"Sure." Now that his plan was successfully in operation, Bobby agreed heartily to any suggestion from his victim, and even laid a burned match on the milky river that flowed toward the drain. He became engrossed in boat-sailing, with a stopper to dam the unusual lake, and only footsteps in the hall reminded him that he was assisting Tippy in her crime.

"Hurry," he ordered, standing back and folding his arms. "Go upstairs and get your fav'rite doll."

"You mean Georgia?" Tippy asked, and added at his nod, "What's Georgia going to do?"

"You go and get her and you'll find out."

Tippy pattered up the stairs, a stirring of dread in her small mother heart. She feared that Georgia, who usually bore the brunt of things, was apt to have another sad experience. So she smoothed the matted yellow curls tenderly and only yielded her to Bobby after one last tender hug.

"Please be awful careful of her, Bobby," she begged. "She's my oldest child and I'd simply die if anything happened to her."

"Nothin's going to happen to her." Bobby was gruff, and he dangled Georgia by one arm, so like a torturing gangster that Tippy tried to snatch her back.

"You can't do that, Tip," he told her, holding Georgia high above his head. "You've been bad so you've gotta be good. You've got to be a heroine or you sure will get spanked."

Tippy agreed reluctantly and with heavy heart that she must go on, and for some time the house was very quiet. Penny read a story with one eye on the clock and half of her mind wondering whether her mother would take the car out that afternoon. As the chimes rang four o'clock, the air was filled with blood-curdling shrieks. Penny's magazine sailed into space as Tippy screamed her way along the hall and fell prostrate on the rug. With a swoop Penny dived for her, only to collide with her mother who had hurtled down the stairs.

"What is it?" they both cried as they tried to lift her up. "What's happened, Tippy?"

"It's Georgia," Tippy wailed. "She's dead. Bobby says she is,—way down in the ground in a box."

"Tippy, for heaven's sake!" Mrs. Parrish carried her, a limp bundle, to a chair and smoothed back the curls from her swollen face. "Georgia can't die. She's just a doll. So try to tell us what happened."

"I don't want to be a hair—hair—something." Tippy clutched her mother around the neck. She was pressed so close against Mrs. Parrish's shoulder that the two heads bent above her had to strain to catch the muffled words. "Bobby buried Georgia," she sobbed, "so that I could be what Penny is. But I don't *want* ice cream. I just want Georgia. And now she's under the rose bush, all cold and dead."

"No, she isn't, Tippy." Penny took her turn at the coddling. She carried the forlorn young mother along the hall, a chain of sobs and shrieks firecrackering along behind them, while Mrs. Parrish snatched up coats and sweaters. "She's all right."

But when they reached the rose bush under which Georgia was supposed to lie in state, she wasn't all right. She wasn't even there. A gaping hole suggested a hastily dug grave, bits of shoe box and pink dress were evidence of a recent burial— but of the victim there was no sign.

"Woofy's got her!" Penny yelled above Tippy's renewed screams. "Here Woofy, Woofy, Woofy!"

Mrs. Parrish ran in circles about the yard, adding her calls to the din. "Oh, my goodness," she kept saying as she stopped to look in impossible places. "How far do you suppose he's gone?"

"Not far." Penny bundled Tippy into a coat before she raced across a neighbor's lawn and into a deserted playhouse. Snarls and yelps came from the dusky interior as she squeezed through the door, and the front half of Woofy lay spread before her like an old fur rug while his tail waved plumily in the air. He was yapping joyfully at what had once been Georgia.

"You beast!" Penny cried, giving him a push and snatching up the doll. "You should be ashamed of yourself."

She inspected the bedraggled remains of a blue-eyed beauty, and Woofy grinned up at her. Georgia was definitely a sight. She stared back at Penny in a dazed way until with a despairing clunk, her eyes disappeared somewhere into her middle where they rattled hollowly.

"Good grief." Penny smoothed a wad of yellow curls that fell off in her hand and shook Georgia until she disgorged her eyes. Mindful of the commotion that still raged in her own yard, she found a soiled rag, stuffed it into Georgia's yawning cranium until her sight was restored, then clapped her hair back on. A few pulls and jerks at twisted clothing and she tore back into the din.

"Here she is," she called. "We'll go in the house and fix her up until she's as good as new."

Tippy's tears changed to smiles, but Penny was careful that Georgia reentered her world high above a little face that stared up critically. Georgia wasn't ready, yet, for close inspection.

"What do you suppose has become of Bobby?" Mrs. Parrish asked when Penny had repeated the conversation about heroines.

"I don't know; but he won't show up for a while." Penny, busy with glue and scissors and pink material, looked up with a grin. "He's taken himself far, far away. I'll bet. . . ." She turned her eyes to the door where Trudy stood, starched and worried in her big white apron.

"There ain't no milk for the children's supper," Trudy announced. "Do you s'pose Mr. David's been over here and dranken it?"

"No." Mrs. Parrish shook her head and hid a smile. "It's a long story, Trudy, and I'll tell it to you this evening, but it leaves the children a bit out of luck because I'd planned oatmeal for them. I think, under the circumstances . . ." she looked at Tippy, solemn and unhappy in her chair . . . "I think that shredded wheat would be much tastier."

"Oh, dear."

Tippy burst into tears, but her mother calmly threaded a needle for Penny and winked at Trudy. "Just give them dry shredded wheat with sugar," she insisted.

"Yas'm." Trudy's face was bland. The Parrishes, unpredictable as they were, never puzzled her. "They're my family," she always said and, after fifteen years with them, would have jumped from the housetop at their bidding, sure that they would catch her and sure they had an excellent reason for their request.

"I got something on my conscience, though," she volunteered as she folded her hands above her apron. "It's about the coffee pot I broke."

"Trudy," Marjorie Parrish sat up straight and stared at her. "Please don't have a conscience—not today."

"No'm. But I've been thinkin' I ought to take my church money for a new one. I've been savin' it right regular."

"I know you have." Mrs. Parrish got up and went to put her arm around the straight narrow shoulders. "You go on saving it. And if you want to smash every piece of china we have, please, please don't get conscience-stricken about it. Just smash and be happy." She turned Trudy toward the hall as the front door slammed and her husband's voice boomed:

"Hey! Is anybody home around here?"

She hurried to him, eager to explain the afternoon before he encountered the mess in the sun room, but he was too quick for her. "Do you know what I did today?" he asked after a hasty kiss. "Of all the stupid, idiotic things . . ."

"Oh, please don't say it, Dave." Her hand reaching for his mouth was caught in both of his.

"Well, you'd better hear it now because you're going to have a darning job to do. Just look at that." He threw open his olive drab short coat to display a jagged burn that reached the full length of a patch pocket. "I stuck my pipe in, thinking it was out, and the matches exploded. I swear I'm going to give up smoking."

"Don't you dare!" She collapsed on the bottom step of the stairway and burst into laughter. "This is all too ridiculous!" she cried. "Sit down here a minute."

"But my pocket!"

"I don't care about your pocket. I'll mend it, but listen to this."

She began an account of the troublesome family consciences and, as they sat side by side on the step, her words were mingled with chuckles interspersed with rumbling questions. Yates, his arms laden with boots, saw them sitting there, wondered how to get by them, and finally back-tracked down the hall.

"Hey, Yates!" Major Parrish heard him and leaned around the newel post to ask: "Have you broken, forgotten, or left anything undone today?"

"No, sir!"

"You're sure, now? Think before you speak."

"No, sir! I done everything Miz Parrish told me to."

Yates's brow was furrowed but his gaze was steadfast. "I know I has."

"Then you're a man to be congratulated." Major Parrish grinned approval at him and warmed the colored man's heart by adding, "You're the only member of the family who has had a perfect day."

"Thank you, sir." Yates drew himself into stiff attention, slightly hampered by his boots, and marched off in soldierly fashion.

"You forgot me." Marjorie Parrish's voice was small as she turned the spotlight on herself. "You didn't ask me what I've done."

"I don't need to." Her husband looked slyly at her. "I know."

"What was it?"

"Mrs. Parrish." He put his arm around her shoulder and pulled her to him. "This afternoon," he whispered, "I discovered that, while our right rear fender is not broken, it is very badly bent."

"It *is?*"

"It most certainly is."

"My goodness!" She leaned against him and giggled. "I did it this morning," she admitted, "and, until everyone got so noble, I had planned to sneak off and have it fixed. Listen, what was that?"

"That" was a thin treble that could belong only to Bobby. It came from the kitchen, and the two on the stairway looked at each other. "What shall we do about him?"

Major Parrish laughed and got up. "There has been so much talk around here of heroines," he said, "that I think I had better take our young son upstairs and explain what a hero is. Give us fifteen minutes alone together and for the next few weeks, I promise you, Bobby will put even Penny in the shade."

CHAPTER VIII

A DOUBTFUL THANKSGIVING

After the general eruption of consciences, the Parrish family jogged along undramatically and, for them, calmly. Penny dragged herself out of bed each morning and faced the early darkness with yawning shivers, and the rest of the family refrained from offering her their sympathy. The Thanksgiving turkey arrived from Gladstone Farms, some twenty-odd pounds of him, garnished with a bunch of parsley clasped like a bouquet to his fat chest and paper frills hiding his loss of lower limbs. David or Michael or Dick telephoned at every opportunity to add their suggestions for the dinner menu or to reiterate that they would arrive upon the dot; and Trudy baked and was happy.

"Hot dog!" Penny said on Thanksgiving morning as she dusted and thumped tires in the cold garage. "You're mine again, my proud beauty. I'll take you out for a spin."

She bowled around the Post, hoping that a few of her friends might be braving the cold and, as she passed the club, looked intently at a lone figure standing on the steps. He looked odd on a Post that bristled with uniforms, for he was bundled into a heavy overcoat, and the muffler that almost met the rakish gray fedora left but a glimpse of a face that was familiar.

"Hi, Lieutenant Hayes," she called, stopping the car. "What are you doing here?"

"Hello, Penny. I'm the forgotten man."

He came down the steps and Penny's heart did its usual thumping as the youngest, handsomest second lieutenant in the Army grinned at her.

"I came up to spend Thanksgiving with Grace and Harry Campbell, but Grace got word that her mother is ill,—so they pulled out and left me. How are you?"

"I'm fine. Hop in and I'll take you home with me."

"I couldn't do that."

"Sure, you could. You haven't any plans, have you?"

"None in particular. I was going to collect some of the first classmen I know as soon as they get out of church."

"Pooh. They'll all be off on long week-ends. David and Dick and Michael will be over home."

"They will? I'd like to see them. Sure I wouldn't make one too many?"

"Of course not. Carrol Houghton and her father are coming, too."

"Is that the pretty girl who visited you at Arden?"

"Umhum." Penny's eyes twinkled as she watched his face quicken into interest, and she opened the door. "Hop in."

"I have my car."

"Well, ride in mine. It's new, and it's been in hock to the family for a couple of weeks."

"Same old Penny, aren't you?" he teased as he swung himself in beside her. "Honest and outspoken."

"Why not?" She laughed as she threw the car in gear. "Golly, when I think of the way we pestered you at Arden. . . . Why, once I even picked up a gum wrapper that you dropped! All we wanted was to admire you from a distance."

"And you embarrassed me no end. Fresh out of the Point, and nervous and scared to death." He turned in the seat and faced her. "You've grown up, Penny."

"I hope not." She swung around a corner and waved to a passing car. "I'm rising sixteen, but it's a long time away. How old are you?"

"Twenty-two. Twenty-three come the second of January. But that's a long time away, too."

"Not so far,—and it still makes you *mighty* old. You can sit with Mums and Dad after dinner."

"I will not." He grinned at her as she flicked him an amused glance, and touched her sleeve with a gloved hand. "A bit dressed up, aren't you, for just a ride around the Post alone?"

"Um, it's my new suit. Pretty, isn't it?" She patted the fur and added smugly: "I haven't worn it since the evening I was with Jimmie Stewart and Katharine Hepburn."

"Since you were with *whom?*"

"With some stars I know." She enjoyed his surprise for almost a block, then relented. "I'll tell you the story," she offered, "if you'd like to ride out around the reservoir."

"Sister, drive on. I'm dying of curiosity."

As they rolled along, crunching over frozen ruts but snug with their heater, Penny related her magic day in New York. Terry Hayes was turned toward her and he listened with flattering interest.

"Gosh, Pen," he said when she had finished, "you had yourself a time; and you certainly can tell about it. Did you ever try to write?"

"Not yet." Penny laughed, then added confidently: "But someday I will. I'm going to write, and I'm going to act."

"I'll bet you do. You're a funny kid."

The car stopped in the Parrish drive and he opened the door and held out his hand to her. "Someday I'll be awfully proud to say 'I knew her when.'"

Penny sighed as she slid across the seat. "Maybe you will," she said with a shake of her head, "but it's a long time off."

"That doesn't matter." He leaned against the car door and looked down at her. "Right now you're having fun."

"I'm having a grand time." Penny banged the door shut and grinned. "And really I'm in no hurry. But you're right, my friend; someday you're going to say 'I knew her when.'"

They slithered along the drive and Penny led the way through the garage. "Yoo-hoo," she called from the side hall. "I've brought another guest."

"Who is it?" her mother's voice answered over the stair rail.

"Guess." Penny motioned toward the coat closet and went to look upward. "He's very young, tall, has hair the color of David's, and devasting blue eyes. He's got the kind of chin that could stick out when he's mad," she turned with an impudent wink, "if he ever gets mad—and his nose is nice and straight. He used to be at Fort Arden and now he's on Governors Island. He . . ."

Her voice ended in a gulp as a hand clapped over her mouth and Terry Hayes looked up at Mrs. Parrish. "You should teach your child not to embarrass people," he growled. "She's much too pert. Hello, Mrs. Parrish."

"Hello, Terry." She hurried down the stairs, holding out her hand. "It's so nice to see you. Where did Penny find you?"

"Standing forlornly on the club steps. I do hope I'm not intruding on a family day."

"We're thrilled to have you, Dave!" Mrs. Parrish went back a step or two and called her husband. "Hurry down. Terry Hayes is here."

"Coming." Major Parrish ran down, and met a hesitant handclasp with a firm grip. "Glad to see you, boy. We can always trust Penny to bring us pleasant surprises. Come into the sun room."

From then on at intervals, blasts of cold air filled the hall. The three cadets stormed in, yelling for food and a look at the turkey, and fell upon the surprise guest with friendly claps on the shoulder. The children, the dog, and a stray cat were brought in, put out and brought in again so many times, that the door wagged on its hinges.

"Where under the sun are the Houghtons?" Penny kept worrying. "Carrol said they'd be here by twelve."

"They're coming. I hear the horn." David shot past her to the garage. "Move that rattle-trap of yours out of the way, Pen," he shouted. "They can't get into the drive."

"Okay. Rattle-trap, indeed." Penny steered her darling into its accustomed berth and slid back to Carrol's coupé. I think Dad ought to take our big car out of the garage," she said as she poked her head through the window. "Then the two friends could stand side by side all day. Why were you so late?"

"We had a telephone call from Grandmother. She wants me to go to Florida with her for the Christmas holidays."

"You aren't going, are you?" David peered around Penny, and Carrol shook her head.

Mr. Houghton leaned across her and looked at David solemnly. "Thanks for helping me keep her here," he said. "I think you had more to do with it than I did."

"Boy!" David shuddered. "She almost scared me to death. Come inside, we have a treat for you."

"What?"

Carrol was climbing out and Mr. Houghton and Major Parrish were unloading packages, that to Penny, who had provided the treat, looked more intriguing.

"The great Hayes is here."

"No!" Carrol stopped on the brown lawn in amazement. "Do you mean the officer who scared me silly the night of the scavenger hunt when I had to ask him for his lieutenant's bar?"

"The very same. Penny brought him home. But he's really a swell guy."

The "swell guy" looked up with interest as Carrol came into the room. "I don't suppose you remember me," he said as he went to meet her. "I'm the chap who gave you the gold bar and tried to date you for a dance."

"I remember. And you're the chap who showed me your pen and ink drawing of a horse. It was a very nice horse," she explained to the others, "or would have been if it had had two hind legs and a tail."

"It finally got 'em. You know, I sold it to a magazine."

Carrol sat down on the divan and, still extolling the beauty of his horse, he followed her. He rumpled his hair as he talked, and while he flung glances at the others now and then, his conversation had the definite intimacy of a tête-à-tête.

"Look," Dick said, when he could break into a split-second pause, "speaking of dances—how about the New Year hop?"

"Who was speaking of dances?" Terry's eyebrows lifted with his voice and without waiting for an answer he added, "I get it. You know, that ought to be a good hop. I'm planning to come up for it."

"For a *plebe* hop? Listen." Dick was plainly irked and Terry Hayes enjoyed it. "You wouldn't leave your public to come up and watch a bunch of plebes get their only break of the year."

"Why not? Maybe I could be a chaperon."

"Huh!"

"Well, I might. Are you girls dated up?" He turned quickly to Carrol. "What about you?"

"I'm dragging David." Carrol's eyes held mirth but they held a wariness, too. "We planned that—way last summer. And Pen has Michael, and all the girls we know have dates. So I expect you'll have to do the best you can with little old New York and all the night spots."

"I never can date you for a dance." Terry folded his arms and shot a glower at David. "What's he got that I haven't?" he demanded.

"Not a thing." Penny was gleeful at his discomfiture. "Except that you're too old."

"You can't repeat things, son," Michael admonished him. "You were a plebe five years ago, and you had your fun. What's become of the little girls you knew then?"

"They got married. Nobody wanted me." He leaned back comfortably, the center of attention again, but David cut his pleasure short.

"Mums and Dad and Uncle Lang are banging ping-pong balls in the basement," he said. "Shall we go down?"

The Thanksgiving dinner with Yates and Trudy in command was flawless. Conversation outlasted appetites and no one was happier than Trudy as she wedged a well-picked turkey carcass into a covered pan and watched Yates cut wide triangles of mince pies.

"'Twas sho' good to see them boys eat," she ruminated over and over as she cleared the table and stole glances at the somnambulistic occupants of the living-room. "They's so full they's a-walking and a-talking in their sleep."

They seemed to be. The elder diners, definitely, had yawning desires for a good magazine and a soft bed, and groaned in unison at David's suggestion of a brisk walk through the woods.

"No, thank you," Langdon Houghton said, stretching his long legs toward cheerful flames and reaching for his pipe. "I rode a horse this morning. You kids run on if you like."

In the end only six wrapped themselves in heavy coats and braved the cold. Penny danced along between Dick and Michael, and Carrol brought up the rear with David and Terry Hayes.

"How's school?" Terry asked.

"Pretty tough, but okay." David was laconic in his answer. He was looking at Carrol's curls against the red lining of her cream wolf parka and wishing he could swing along beside her, holding the red mitten that was thrust into the pocket of her wolf coat.

"Are they hazing you a lot?"

"Some. See that rabbit over there, Carrol?" He laid a detaining hand on her arm but Terry Hayes stopped also, so he pushed her gently on again. "You should have Penny tell

you the story about meeting the movie stars," he suggested
hopefully. "She had quite a day."

"She told me about it this morning." Unmindful of the
hint, Terry leaned toward Carrol and asked softly, "Warm
enough?"

"I'm fine. It's wonderful out, isn't it?" She took a deep
breath of the clear cold air that smelled of future snow, and
Terry snatched the conversation again.

"You know, this reminds me of one time when I was a
cadet," he said to her as though David weren't there. "A
bunch of us came up this way one Sunday afternoon. And
when we got way out by the stadium a cold, sleety rain began. My wife had just got out of the hospital, so . . ."

"Your *what?* I didn't know you were married." Carrol's
attention was caught.

"My wife, my roommate. He'd had flu. He was supposed
to be confined to quarters, and I knew if he got a chill the
word would get around that he was off limits, and he'd get a
quill for it. So . . ."

"Wait a minute." Carrol laughed up at him, enjoying his
patter, but puzzled by its meaning. "I know what 'off limits'
is, because every interesting place seems to be 'off limits' for
a plebe, but what's a quill?"

"It's a skin, a demerit. I didn't realize how the old lingo
would come back if I got up here again. It's fun to talk it."
He reached for her arm and rattled on, as oblivious of David
as of the brown trees and the cold, dead leaves under foot.
"My wife was a hivey—the studious type—and I was sort
of fond of the cuss. So I piled my sweater on him and we
began a double time."

His voice went on and on like the path they were climbing, and Carrol's questions brought such lengthy explana-
tions that David ceased to listen or to stop when they paused
for a backward glance at the Post below them.

"David, wait a minute," Carrol called as he strode on toward Dick, who was kneeling to tie his shoe. But her voice was blown away on the wind and Terry turned her back to the view again. "Do him good for me to beat his time," he told her. "Her's a cocky young pup."

"Not half as cocky as you are." Carrol looked levelly at him. "David's not cocky. He just thinks we don't want him."

"Do we?"

"I do. And I don't like to hurt people's feelings. Let's go on."

"Okay. But wait until I light a cigarette."

The search for case and matches, the stubborn refusal of the flame to brave the wind, took so long that the foursome ahead had disappeared around a curve before Carrol's sturdy brogues were hurrying after them. The patter that accompanied her, that delayed her, had lost its charm and her interest was only on the winding way before her.

"We aren't lost, are we?" she asked anxiously as the woods became dusky and still. "The road to the post should come in about here."

"It does; right there through the trees. And it isn't late."

"I know it, but the boys will have to go back to barracks pretty soon. I want to see them before they go."

But hurry as fast as she could, the house was quiet when she reached it. "Where are the boys?" she called as she dashed through the door, leaving Terry Hayes to come in or stay out as he liked.

"They just left." Penny, poking the dying fire, turned around. "They still wanted to walk, so they trudged off."

"I'll be back in a minute."

As Carrol dashed for the side hall and the garage, Penny dropped the poker and called after her: "Take my car. The keys are above the windshield; and the family went off in yours."

The bang of the door answered her and she glared at Terry who was leaning against the wall, grinning. "You're a fine guest," she said with a frown. "Just look at all the trouble you've made."

"*Me?* I haven't made any trouble."

"You have, too. David counted on a nice day and then you had to go and turn on all that charm that used to fool us kids." She picked up the poker to make vicious stabs at the igniting logs and Terry came over to her.

"Don't I fool you now?" he demanded.

"Not one bit." Penny's voice was scornful as she looked at him. "Carrol was being nice to you because you were our guest,—but you were only showing off."

"That's pretty unkind, Pen."

"Well, *you* were unkind." She faced him, straight and stubborn. "You knew you were butting in on David and you didn't care. You're an officer, so you thought you could take advantage of a poor little fourth classman."

"And now you don't like me so much?"

"No." Her eyes were honest and unforgiving. "I used to think you were a hero. But now I don't like you nearly so much."

"That's funny." Terry gave her a long, keen look. "It's very funny. Because now I like you more."

Without another word he turned and walked out of the house, leaving her, for the first time in her life, speechless.

Carrol, swinging the car over the icy ruts, was watching for three gray-coated figures. They were striding along Thayer Road, almost to Grant Hall, when her headlights found them. She slowed the car, saw Dick trotting a little to keep up with the long steps of David and Michael, and without knowing what she did, pressed the foot brake to the floor. Her eyes followed them until they disappeared inside their barracks, then she turned the car around to drive slowly back along the way she had come.

"There wasn't anything I could say," she told Penny, giving her the car keys. "Not before the others. Do you think

David really minded?" She took off her parka and smoothed the fur absently.

"I guess he did." Penny sighed before she continued. "He was pretty quiet. But sometimes David is, you know."

"I know, but . . ." Carrol threw the parka on a chair and sat down before the fire. "I was rude," she said, watching the sparks dance up the chimney. "But I didn't mean to be. The trouble is, Pen, we aren't old enough to handle situations. Terry Hayes is a man. And if I'd been older I'd have put him in his place and managed things."

"Well, *I* did; put him in his place, I mean." Penny looked at the brass rod she still held in her hand. "I was so mad I almost hit him with the poker. I refrained—but I did tell him off."

"Why, Penny Parrish!"

"Wasn't it awful?" Penny looked pleased in spite of her self-condemnation. "I finished up Thanksgiving day with a bang."

"Was he mad?"

"I guess so. I don't know. He acted kind of queer."

She related the conversation as best she could, and Carrol pushed her own troubles into the background to listen. "It's all ridiculous," she said as Penny finished with a belligerent wave of her weapon. "If it weren't for David we could laugh about it. I wouldn't hurt David for the world."

"I know it. Shall we call him up after supper hour?"

"I don't think so." Carrol shook her head. "When I can I'll talk to him. But I believe that he'll reason it out. David's pretty sane, you know. And after all, when you come right down to it, *he* walked off and left me."

"That's right. He did."

"And it isn't as though I *liked* Lieutenant Hayes."

"Oh, he's definitely a mess."

"So . . ." Carrol threw out her hands and the dimple at the corner of her mouth twitched, "we'll wait and see what David does."

"It won't hurt him." Penny was philosophical in her diagnosis of David. "He's kind of cocky sometimes and it will be good for him to worry about you a little."

She went to pull Carrol to her feet and, in spite of protest, propelled her to the kitchen. "Even if we aren't hungry," she coaxed, "let's just see if there's any white meat sticking to the turkey."

CHAPTER IX

INSIDE BARRACKS

David laid the cake of soap in a meticulous line with his tooth brush, straightened the two towels that hung side by side, and began to dust the tin lamp shades that covered the student lamps above the desks. Michael, dismantling his bed, looked up from the mattress he was rolling into a neat cylinder.

"You're pretty quiet this morning," he mentioned as he settled the mattress on the foot of his army cot where it would provide no temptation to a weary body. "Hayes still got your goat?"

"I'd like to wring his neck." David squinted into the lampshade for any betraying spot of dust that might cost three demerits and turned to inspect the shoes that stood in a polished row beneath his bunk. He sat down on a hard, wooden chair, careful of the crease in his trousers, while Michael gave his locker one more careful inspection.

"Talked to Carrol, yet?" he asked as he straightened a neat pile of undershirts.

"No."

"You're taking it too hard. Forget it. Carrol's okay."

"Sure, I know that." David thumbed through a geometry book, selected a pencil and his notebook and was in the act of indulging in a large and hearty sigh, when the door was flung open.

"Mr. Dumbjohn."

"Yes, sir." David jumped up, threw out his chest until his elbows were but a few inches apart behind him, drew his chin into the braid on his collar, and stood at rigid attention.

"You look too happy this morning." The upper classman who had burst in upon his privacy glared at him. "Wipe off that smile."

"Yes, sir." David passed a hand over his face and returned to his pose.

"And you, Mr. Dooflicket." The tormentor cast a critical eye upon Michael. "Get your shoulders back. I said *back!*" he ordered as the buttons on Michael's blouse strained from the pull. "Don't you know what back is, Mr. Dooflicket?"

"Yes, sir."

"Elucidate."

"Back is the opposite of front, sir. To or toward the rear; behind."

"Then get 'em back."

A bugle sounded and he disappeared as suddenly as he had come.

"Ready?" Michael asked, releasing his shoulders as calmly as if nothing unusual had occurred. "I'll set your card for you. What do you have first?"

"Math."

David selected the necessary impedimenta for classroom work as Michael adjusted the two charts that hung on the wall. They told the exact location of a cadet for every hour of the day and also led to heavy punishment if the inspecting tactical officer, known familiarly as a Tac, discovered them unmarked.

"Who's going first, you or me?" David asked.

"I'll take it." Michael went to the door and turned to add, "Don't run over me on the stairs."

They began a dog-trot down the hall, obeying the rule of the Point that all plebes must double-time through halls and must take the stairs two at a time, making their exit only from the basement doors. Michael shot through the door first, followed by a flash of David, and as they pulled up to go their separate ways, they were two odd caricatures, strutting their courses with fixed stares and wheeling sharply at all corners. The morning was a busy one and the tingling little worry that was Carrol was pushed far back in David's mind. Bells rang and bugles blew. He joined his section and was marched stiffly to other classes; he recited, wrote on blackboards, marched again, and eventually found himself back in his own bare cubicle.

Promptly at noon he hurtled himself into the street again; joined the column that was his battalion and, with the roll of drums and the blare of trumpets, marched to the fortress-like structure known as the mess hall. There, like scurrying beetles, the plebes left their ranks to trot through the doors and to their tables; and David, after disposing of his overcoat and cap in a rack beneath his chair, stood erect and expectant with a downward view of a few feet of tablecloth, his plate and his flat silver.

"Take seats!" The First Captain shouted the command, and David slid onto three inches of chair and tried to see over his chest. A platter of meat was set before him and, with an inaudible sigh, he realized he was "gunner" again and would do the carving, while the other two plebes at the table were only water or coffee "corporals."

"Mr. Dumbjohn, will you tell us how many days there are until Christmas?"

Sensing the stern eye that was directed at him, David hacked at a stubborn slice of beef that refused to leave the roast and intoned as evenly as he could: "There are twenty-eight days and a butt until Christmas, sir."

Silence greeted his information and a first classman complained to the dining room at large: "Mr. Dumbguard is slow with his carving; he must read the book on etiquette."

Several heads nodded in unison and fists began pounding for the corporals to hurry with their pouring. Glad of a respite, David sawed away and hoped that he would be al-lowed to eat his dinner with a fair amount of peace. He was lifting his first forkful when the onslaught came.

"Mr. Dumbell, have you ever seen an Ethiopian?"

"No, sir." David, his eyes on his plate, laid down his fork.

"Have you ever heard an Ethiopian talk?"

"No, sir."

"Well, Mr. Dumbell, if you *had* heard an Ethiopian talk— just what is your idea of how the conversation would sound?"

David began a lingo that he hoped would pass for the correct thing in Ethiopian dialect and was allowed to proceed for some time. At last, when his food had become cold on his plate and his voice hoarse from competing with the chatter that went on around him, the upper classmen returned their empty plates to him and decided that Mr. Dumbjohn and Mr. Dooflicket should attempt better imitations of an Ethiopian. When the roast was but a nub on its plate, he gulped what food he had time for and, with downcast eyes and cramped muscles, bolted a piece of pie.

"Mr. Dumbunny's table manners are bad." The yearling

who leaned toward him and whom he had known all his life, was one of his ablest tormentors. "Will you see if the goldfish is in the pitcher today, Mr. Dumbunny?"

"Yes, sir." David plunged his hand into the ice water and stirred about tentatively. "It isn't there today, sir." Chillingly, he wished that someday it *would* be there—for nothing would have given him greater pleasure than to pull out and display a bright yellow fish.

He dried his hand on his napkin, cast his eyes reverently upon his plate again and, at a signal, arose with the others. His stiff trot returned him to his battalion and on his trumpeted march to barracks he counted that his noon meal, while sustaining, had been only one of the five hundred and sixty-four milestones he must pass before June freed him.

"It's four o'clock," Michael said some hours later, throwing his books on his study table and draping himself on his hard chair. "Going over home for your free half hour?"

"No." David, on his spine in the other chair, shook his head. "It only makes me soft and makes things harder to take. The table commandant invited me to give a little skit tonight for the delectation of my soupmates, on my joyous Thanksgiving. Joyous nuts!"

"I got one, too."

"What are you going to tell 'em?"

"There isn't much I can tell 'em—I have to be the turkey." Michael slumped lower, practising his gobble, while David yawned and prepared for an upright nap.

"Hi, pals." Dick's red head was thrust inside the door. "I got all the way up here without a single upper classman hailing me. Okay to come in?"

"Come on in." Michael shifted from his chair to his desk and Dick closed the door softly. "Overheard a little gossip," he said as he curved his spine into a better arc than David's. "Some of the guys have got wind that the great Hayes is on the Post."

"What of it?" David slewed around to glare. "A bunch of the first classmen were friends of his a year ago."

"Yeah, I know it. But it seems he mentioned one Thanksgiving dinner with Major and Mrs. Parrish and all the little Parrishes—and also one beautiful but young blond femme who was visiting them. He even said he'd gone off the deep end again."

"The big bum!"

"Now wait a minute." Dick held up his hand for silence. "The guys I overheard said he seemed to be in earnest. Of course, I was busy trying to find a certain book in the library and had to keep moving around so that I missed a bit, but the general idea that I gathered was this: The two bright boys have done some figuring. They've noticed Carrol flitting around, too. So . . ." Dick sat up straighter and shook his head sadly at David . . . "you're in for some rough going tonight."

"I won't do it." David got up and stalked around the room. "I'll get a dining permit and make Dad take me to the hotel to eat with a long lost cousin, or something."

"A D.P. won't help you. You'd only catch it tomorrow in a double dose. No, my son," Michael leaned back and grinned at David, "all you can do is to be as clever as you can and tell all without telling anything. I've decided I'm lucky to be a turkey." He gobbled again for Dick's approval and went to his locker. "Dress parade in twenty minutes," he said, tossing a pair of stiff cuffs on his desk. "Better start getting ready."

"I'm on my way." Dick lounged to the door and flicked a hand at David. "Good luck, old man," he saluted. "I'll be around to get the low-down."

David marched stiffly through parade. As he wheeled and turned, halted and stood for the review, his mind was on the next hour and he wondered how much he could tell and how much keep hidden. Penny was among the spectators, and when he returned his cap and overcoat to his locker he was not surprised to be called to the telephone.

"Hello," Penny's voice greeted him over the wire. "I was glad to notice this afternoon that you're still alive. Why haven't you been over home this week?"

"No could do."

"Carrol was here yesterday."

"Was she?"

"Terry Hayes called her up in New York and asked her and her father out to dinner."

"That's nice."

"David!" Penny gave the phone on her end of the line a shake and her words were garbled. Then—"Are you mad at Carrol?" her words came back.

"Of course not."

"Well, why don't you *do* something? My goodness, David, Carrol's all upset and worried to death because she thinks you're mad at her, and you didn't come over home; and what with Terry hanging around . . ."

"Sorry. Have to go now, Pen. Tell Mums that I'll be over soon. Good-by."

David hung the receiver back on its hook, his face thoughtful. He stood for some seconds in the orderly room, wondering what chance he could have, a fourth classman, against a dashing young officer with time and money to spend. "It's no use butting in," he told himself. "Carrol's a swell girl but I haven't a darn thing to offer. I can't even take her to dances! So why should she want to sit around and *look* at me!"

He decided to eliminate himself from the picture, completely, and hurried back to his bare haven. Mess call sounded while he was expounding his noble intentions to Michael, and he joined the hungry marchers with a lump of cold dread crowding out his appetite.

"Mr. Dumbcracker," a hated voice began as he struggled with the coffee pitcher, "we understand that your family entertained quite lavishly on Thanksgiving day. Will you favor us with an account of that festive occasion?"

"Yes, sir."

"We'd like you to stand, Mr. Dumbcracker."

David got to his feet and, with lowered eyes, began his recital. "It was a very enjoyable day, sir," he proclaimed. "The weather was cold but clear as my wife, a brother plebe and I went to accept the invitation of my parents. Before dinner we played a very exciting set of ping pong with hard-won games for each team." He hoped to devote as much time and attention as he could to the ping-pong game and was pleased when his trap caught a voice.

"Did you cheer, Mr. Dumbjohn?"

"Oh yes, sir."

"Will you favor us with a cheer?"

David put his heart and soul into several hoorays that, although they were deafening, brought no notice from the other tables and no help from the officer in charge who sat grandly on his balcony, staring down on the two long wings of dining room—but seeing nothing.

"It was very poor cheering and I'm sure the table will agree with me."

There followed a conference on his powers as a cheer leader, with most uncomplimentary remarks and, after a noisy vote, he was black-balled as a future candidate for the team. He listened intently, hoping to be asked for a second exhibition, but his heart sank when he was invited to continue his story.

"I understand you had other guests for the day," the table commandant prompted him. "We should like to hear about that, too."

"We had some friends of my parents and sister, sir."

"A recent graduate of the Academy, I believe,—and a very pretty young lady?"

"Yes, sir."

"*Mr. Dumbjohn!*" The fist that pounded the table sent the water corporal grabbing for his pitcher. "When I ask for an account of your day I expect an entertaining account. Please entertain us."

"Very well, sir." David began again, carefully inserting details but eliminating personalities and expounding on the superb qualities of the turkey, the dessert and the pleasantly upholstered chairs.

"He had too much ease," his hated childhood playmate, Bill Henderson, said across the table. "Did you sit in the comfortable chairs all afternoon, Mr. Dumbjohn?"

"No, sir." Knowing what answer was expected and believing it would be better to make it than be prodded, David added sparingly, "We went for a walk."

"The entire family went with you, I presume?"

"No, sir—just my sister and her friend, my wife, my friend and the officer."

"Ah—the officer. He isn't a friend?"

"Sir . . ." David took a deep breath and plunged. "It would be most unseemly for me, a lowly plebe, to think of myself as being the friend of a graduate of the Academy and a lieutenant in the United States Army. He is a respected acquaintance, sir."

Several heads nodded approval and one difficult moment was passed.

"But your sister's friend. She is not above your aspirations?" A taunting voice flung him a cue.

"As a fourth classman, sir, I have no aspirations."

"And no *jealousy*, Mr. Dumbjohn? No jealousy during your walk in the woods or for the interest your 'respected acquaintance' showed for your sister's friend—whom, I might add, we have often noticed in your modest company?"

David's muscles twitched but he remained calm and outwardly untouched as he answered gravely: "I have no jealousy, sir. I have no aspirations and no jealousy. I have only my duty as a cadet."

"And you consider that duty important, Mr. Dumbjohn?"

"No, sir. As a plebe I am not important."

"Just what do you rank, Mr. Dumbjohn—as a plebe?"

"Sir," David's shoulders ached but he felt himself to be on firmer ground, so he recited glibly: "I rank the Superintendent's dog, the Commandant's cat, the waiters in the mess hall, the Hell cats and all the Admirals in the whole blamed Navy."

"You may be seated, Mr. Dumbflicket."

"Thank you, sir." David slid onto his alloted three inches of chair and heartily attacked his dinner, every bite of which was choking him. He was careful to ask for a second glass of milk and seemingly to enjoy the food he forced down his throat. But when he had been marched back to his barracks and been dismissed, he stood for some minutes looking up at the stars. They looked very far away and he felt lonely and very, very small beneath them.

"Hello, David."

His eyes came down to a gray blur before him and he stared at an outstretched hand. It was the hand of fellowship, the treasured recognition of an upper classman, and above it was the smiling face of Bill Henderson.

"Gosh, Bill." David's hand shot out to meet it. "Gosh, you're swell."

"Well, *you* were swell, boy. And you got away with it. Even I couldn't think of anything more to rag you about and I had to tell you so." He grinned and gave David's shoulder a thump. "I'll be a pain in the neck to you tomorrow, but I had to recognize you tonight. So long."

"So long."

David sprang up the stairs, two at a time. "It was okay, Mike," he said breathlessly as he closed the door behind him. "It must have been, because Bill Henderson gave me the hand."

"He *did?*" Michael looked up from the radio he was dialing. "That's *swell!* Think we dare put a blanket over this thing while we study?"

"Wouldn't risk it." David flipped the switch and Michael's arm hung over his shoulder.

"You might give Carrol a ring tomorrow," he suggested. "Get everything straightened out."

"Nope." David pulled out his chair, adjusted his back to fit it and graced the desk with his feet. "Things had better ride along for a while." He thought of his talk with Penny and of his decision to keep aloof in his own little niche, and added, "Carrol's happy, and I've got a heck of a week ahead of me."

He buried himself in his book, and such is the life of a West Pointer, that his troubles at dinner, his long, grinding future, and Carrol, were forgotten. She might stand pensively on her wind-swept terrace looking out over the lights, the joys and sorrows of a great city, might send sighs northward up the Hudson; but when 'lights out' sounded, David only crawled into his freshly made bed and muttered, "Gosh, my head aches."

CHAPTER X

SUMMER IN WINTER

The next week seemed interminably long to Penny. She hounded David by phone and by car and offered every bait she could to entice him to the house.

"Now listen, Pen," he said finally via the telephone, "I'm studying like the dickens for some writs and I'm not coming over home, and I'm not going to be pestered to death by you. They'll charge me rent for the orderly room if you don't stop calling."

"But I want to talk to you about Carrol—really talk, I mean."

"There's nothing to talk about. I wrote Carrol my usual Monday letter and had a note from her that . . ."

"Did you *write* to her?"

"Of course."

"Good-by." Penny cut the connection and jiggled the hook for long distance. Her hurry was so great that when only buzzing and snapping answered her she was too irritated to recognize a voice that followed.

"Hello, hello," it said. "I'm trying to get Major Parrish's quarters."

"Carrol! Hey!" Suddenly confronted with a call that was completed before she had put it in, Penny shouted the first thing that came into her head: "Where are you?"

"I'm at Gladstone and I've been ringing you for ages. Can you come over? Daddy and I are going to Florida after all."

"No! Oh, dear. When?"

"Saturday. I only came down for some of my summer clothes. Could you come and spend the night?"

"I'll see." She laid the receiver on the desk and went in search of her mother. "But I'll have to go," she begged against all her mother's arguments. "Carrol's *going away*."

"It's too snowy, dear. I don't mind your missing school tomorrow, but it will be dark soon, and I can't possibly drive you over when I have this rotten cold. Ask Carrol to come here."

"All right, but I don't think she will." Penny went slowly back to the telephone and Mrs. Parrish sneezed along behind her.

"Parker will come for me," Penny said after a brief exchange of words. "He can start right away."

"Then you may go." Mrs. Parrish motioned for the phone and Penny sped to the big closet where traveling bags were kept.

"But I don't *want* you to go to Florida," she kept reiterating when she sat in Carrol's room, watching her pile dresses on the bed.

"And I certainly don't want to. But Grandmother really isn't well, and Daddy says he'll stay down until after Christmas, so there's nothing else to do."

"Don't you hate missing school?"

"Grandmother is bringing Miss Turner with her." Carrol inspected the clothes she had selected and gave them to a maid to press and pack, then went to drop down near Penny. "You remember Miss Turner; she was my governess in Chicago. I do hate to go but . . . well, Grandmother has always been wonderful to me . . . and I owe it to her, Pen."

"I guess you do." Penny studied her shoe thoughtfully. "But what are you going to do about David?" she asked without looking up.

"About David what?"

"Why, about . . . about Thanksgiving day and Terry and . . . oh, straightening things out."

"David and I are straightened out."

"You are?" Penny looked up eagerly, and Carrol smiled.

"Of course. Here's his letter. Want to read it?"

Penny took the letter and ran her eyes over it. "I don't see any straightening out in it," she said glumly as she glanced back over the page. "It's all about his school, and sounds like a daily bulletin of his classes. It's just a lot of blah with a 'nice to have known you' attitude."

"Of course it is." Carrol laughed as she retrieved the letter and laid it on the table. "Someday I'll show it to David."

"Well, my goodness!" Penny looked from the letter to Carrol and back again. "That doesn't sound as if you'd ever get the chance."

"Listen, Penny." Carrol curled up in her chair and hugged her knees. "I know David lots better than you do."

"You can't. I grew up with him and you just met him last summer. He's the most stubborn, conceited . . ."

"No, he isn't. I can read between the lines of that letter and can understand just what David is thinking."

"What's he thinking? I've been trying all week to find out."

"Well," Carrol pulled Penny to her feet. "Let's go in my sitting room and have a cup of cocoa before the fire. There's going to be too much activity in here."

"All right." Penny hurried into the next room, chose a corner of a flowered sofa and, physically comfortable, waited on mental pins and needles.

"In the first place," Carrol continued calmly as she poked a pillow behind her back, "David is having a hard year. I know that, from things he's told me. Living in barracks as a plebe isn't easy, and I think David gets double hazing because his family is on the Post. The cadets don't approve of a pleasant life at home. Then, too, he has to study so hard because he came straight from high school and hasn't had a year of coaching to help him."

"But what has that to do with you?" Penny, the matter-of-fact, was willing to give David his due, and although she nodded she prodded again. "Where do you come in?"

"I don't, darling; that's the point. David mustn't be bothered by girls this year." She laughed at Penny's wide-eyed stare. "I know you think I'm crazy," she added, "but it's like this: David has a complex."

"Oh, he has not." Penny sat up straight. "David never had a complex in his life."

"Well, he has one now. He's been told so often that he's dumb, that he has no rank and no privileges—until he thinks he hasn't. He can take it—from the boys—and if Terry Hayes hadn't got mixed up in things, he wouldn't have realized how little he has to offer a girl."

"Do you suppose he thinks that?"

"I know he does. I told you I know David, Pen."

"I guess you do." Penny was thoughtful as she stared into the fire. "I suppose he does think that graduation is a long time off, and I've been ragging him, too. I told him about Terry asking you out to dinner and, though I told him you didn't go, I sort of mumbled it. I was trying to pep him up—and, poor child, not once did he come back at me." She saw David, his shoulders bent under a load of care, his head in his hands, and emitting fearful private groans. "Maybe I'd better call him up and tell him I understand about it."

"Oh, Penny." Carrol lay back among the pillows and laughed. "If you dare breathe a word of this conversation to him I'll murder you by long distance from Florida."

"But he must be suffering."

"He isn't suffering. He doesn't even know what's the matter with him."

"Well, my goodness." Her admiration for Carrol was flaring high. "I think you're perfectly wonderful to figure it all out, and then keep still about it. I'm going to be awfully nice to him from now on."

Carrol sighed. "I suppose you'll coddle him and tell him how sorry you are for him," she groaned. "And you'll only make him shut up like a clam. I'll tell you what, Penny." She leaned forward, sure her suggestion would appeal to the actress in Penny more than all the words of caution she could extract from a dictionary. "You'll just have to play a part until I come back. Be nice and sisterly; ask his advice about things, and show that you depend on him." She smiled to herself as she visualized Penny turning herself into a clinging vine, and felt sure that David would put her in her place when he got tired of being over-brotherly.

"I'll lean on him like a broken-down cow shed against the barn!" Penny exclaimed as Carrol knew she would. "I'll make him think he's as important as the Secretary of War, or something. I'll . . ." Her plans for the general harassing of David were interrupted by footsteps in the hall. "Hi, Uncle Lang!" she cried as she ran to Langdon Houghton. "What do you mean by taking Carrol away?"

"Can't help it, Pen," he answered with his arm around her. "I felt so badly about her going that I'm tagging along. Why don't you tag, too?"

"Huh?" Penny's mouth fell open but she managed to say: "I'm sorry; I mean, what did you say, Uncle Lang?"

"I said . . ." He gave Carrol a quick kiss as she hung on his other arm. "Hello, honey. I said, why don't you tag along with us?"

"Why . . . why . . ." Penny was stunned but Carrol was hugging them both and pulling them across the room.

"Oh, Daddy!" she cried. "You're perfectly marvelous. How did you ever happen to think of it when I didn't?"

"The Good Fairy suggested it." Langdon Houghton laughed as he was pushed onto the sofa. "Do you remember the Good Fairy, Miss Parrish; the one who insisted that I come to Fort Arden? She popped into my office this afternoon, and now she insists you should go to Florida. Funny old girl, isn't she?"

Penny laughed, then gulped. "I didn't think, when I invented her, that she was going to do nice things for *me*," she stammered. "It's—it's wonderful of you to want me to go, but I . . ."

"But you what?" He reached up for her and pulled her down on the divan. His free arm went around Carrol on her knees beside them, and he looked at the chocolate pot and the unused cups. "There must have been a deep discussion going on," he smiled, "if you forgot to take nourishment."

"What we were talking about is why I can't go," Penny told him earnestly. "I'm needed at home right now. And then of course, it would be kind of expensive."

"Penny Parrish, you know it wouldn't be." Carrol leaned across her father to argue. "You know the Fairy wouldn't let you pay."

"I suppose not. But . . . well, it's David," she blurted out. "I just can't leave David right now."

The two Houghtons hid their smiles as their glances met, and Carrol jumped up to give Penny a hug. "You're a lamb," she said, winking at her father over Penny's shoulder, "a crazy but well-meaning lamb. Let's call up your mother and talk to her."

"I don't know what to do," Penny sighed as Carrol, the matter settled, poured three cups of steaming chocolate. "I want to go—but I was never away from home on Christmas. In fact, I've never been away from the family at all, except the two weeks I visited Aunt Julia."

She looked up at Mr. Houghton with such a woeful, childish expression that he smiled down at her. "We're not going to coax you, Penny," he told her, sensing her bewilderment; the loyalty and devotion to family ties that made her the lovable person that she was. "But if you *will* go down with us, we'll promise to have you home by Christmas Eve."

"And we'll drive over and talk to your mother and father tonight, won't we, Daddy? And we'll even wait another day or two for you to get ready." Carrol's cheeks were pink with excitement and she dropped to her knees beside the sofa. "Oh, Penny," she coaxed, "think of going swimming and having our lessons together! There are gift shops to poke around in, and curio stores . . ."

"And I could do my Christmas shopping." Hesitation was vanishing and Penny's eyes began to shine, too. "I could send back oranges and things."

"Then you *will* go?"

"I'll talk to Mummy and Daddy. If it's all right with them. . . . Golly!" Her cup rattled against its saucer and she set it down with a plop. "I never thought I'd go to Florida," she said solemnly. "I feel awfully queer."

She felt even "queerer" as she expressed it, when she found herself looking through the plate glass window of her compartment into the upturned faces of her mother and father. "Don't try to come home for Christmas," her mother had said before she kissed Penny good-by in the train vestibule. "Wait until Uncle Lang comes up a few days afterward. And, darling, if you get homesick, don't show it. You're having a wonderful trip and you must always know how happy Daddy and I are about it."

"I know it."

She smiled down and waved again, and the train rolled smoothly through the lighted train sheds and out into the night.

The days that followed were halcyon. The Houghton cottage sat on the dunes above the ocean and Carrol and Penny made several trips a day up and down the path that led to the beach.

"It's a cottage just like Gladstone's a farm," Penny said as she sat under a beach umbrella looking up at the turrets and wide porches that were visible through tall poinsettias and the palm trees. "I wonder what kind of a cave your family could concoct?"

"A roomy little lay-out I have no doubt." Carrol, on her back, sifted sand through her fingers. "Are you going to buy that tea set for your mother?"

"I guess so." Penny considered the tea set she had been hovering over for several days. "Do you think it's too expensive?"

"Well, it isn't cheap, but it looks like Aunt Marjorie. You know that tie I saw that was simply made for Dad? I think I'll buy it."

"I would." Penny rolled out into the sunshine, and pillowing her head on her arms, remarked comfortably: "I'm as brown as a piece of bread in a toaster."

The days drowsed by. Madam Houghton, serene and patrician among her pillows on an upstairs porch, asked only for their tea hour and an amusing account of their day. Miss Turner exacted very little, knowing the sand which scattered from their books was as beneficial as the knowledge that seeped into their minds; and Langdon Houghton brought high-lights into their peaceful existence.

"How about some deep sea fishing?" he would call, sure they would find a thrill in the small boat he had chartered. Or, "Would anyone care to join me in a night at the carnival I discovered up the road?"

They fished for tarpon, snatched at rings from hobby-horses, swam and shopped, and tumbled into bed at night, sunk in dreamless slumber.

"I guess I've bought everything," Penny counted, sitting on the wide porch floor surrounded by tissue paper and tinseled ribbon. "There's the tea set and Dad's cigarette case and Tippy's nurse's outfit and Bobby's pistol with the Indian burned into the leather holster—it's cute, isn't it? What are you reading?"

"A note from David." Carrol's back was pressed against the rail and Penny leaned across her packages.

"What a scrawl," she commented amiably. "It looks as if he'd written it in the dark. What does he say?"

"Nothing." Carrol shrugged and reread the few lines. "He just says 'merry Christmas' and that perhaps he won't be able to write for a while because he's so busy. Funny."

She tucked the letter into the pocket of her white playsuit and picked up a box that was marked for Trudy. "What did you get her?" she asked, rattling it. "I've forgotten."

"I just bought her another purse." Penny concentrated on an ornate rosette she was devising and, after a few twists and pulls, laid it in her lap. "I always give her purses but I wish I could give her lots of money to put in them. You know," she picked up the rosette again and studied it thoughtfully, "someday I'm going to say to my grandchildren . . ."

"Umhum. I know. 'Grandmother never would have become a famous actress . . .' "

"Ah, but that's where you're wrong." Penny held up her finger and her eyes twinkled. "I'm going to say 'darlings, Grandmother would never have become rich if she hadn't visited in all the fine houses of your Aunt Carrol.' I'm green-eyed with envy," she finished complacently, "so I shall go out and earn a lot of money."

"It would be just like you." Carrol smiled as Penny tied her rosette on a knobby package that exploded beneath its decoration, popping off Christmas seals like buttons. "Give that mess to me," she demanded, "and go tell Perkins to bring a box so we can send this junk off before you wear it out."

"Happy to oblige." Penny brushed the clippings from her shorts, straddled across the boxes and sang her way indoors.

"Tomorrow will be Christmas," she said several days later, taking Roman candles and sky rockets from the back of the station wagon. "Imagine firecrackers and people running around in fancy costumes on Christmas! My soul! Even the Christmas tree looks kind of pathetic. I bet he wishes he were back up in the Maine woods."

"He probably does; although he only came from Georgia. But he'll be happy tonight when we dress him up in lights and things." Carrol, from long association with Penny's imagination, often found herself giving life to inanimate objects, and now she chuckled as she went indoors with her packages and wondered if 'he' would like the ornaments she carried.

"I'm not being homesick at all, at all," Penny crooned as she followed. "I'm having a *won*-der-ful time."

"That's good. Let's go and ask Daddy if we trim the tree tonight."

They laid their parcels on a table and bounded up the stairs. Penny was chanting "'Twas the night before Christmas" when Carrol halted at the study door. "Sh!" she whispered. "He's telephoning." She laid her finger on her lips and eased open the door.

"I think that's best. Keep me posted," Langdon Houghton was saying. "If there is any change . . ." He heard the slight creak of the door and turned his head. "I'll call tonight," he said, hastily. "Good-by." He replaced the phone and turned with a smile. "Come in, ladies," he invited.

"We got the stuff for the tree, and we want to know what time we trim it." Carrol perched on his desk and slid along the shining mahogany to leave a corner for Penny.

"The decorations are simply dee-vine," Penny exclaimed. "I never *saw* such enormous balls."

"Happy here, Pen? Glad you came?"

"Uncle Lang, I am superlatively enamoured of my fortunate state." Penny stretched out a brown arm to him. "Look at me. I'm just the color of the furniture."

"So you are." He laid his papers in a drawer and smiled

fondly at her. "Suppose you show me the tree," he suggested. "Is it a good one?"

"It's practically perfect."

They ran down the stairs, Penny shouting above the clatter: "Isn't it grand that I'm not homesick?"

She repeated that over and over; gayly while she trimmed the tree; with a catch in her voice when she hung her stocking; and like a prayer as she got into bed. The next morning she resolutely shut out all thought of another tree that would have electric trains and dolls beneath it, and forced back the tears when she spied a box from home, half hidden beneath drooping sparkling branches.

Madam Houghton was helped down the stairs and, comfortable on a chaise longue in the sunshine, she opened the gifts that were hers and admired the ones Penny and Carrol carried to her.

"I'm so overcome I can't breathe," Penny cried as she danced about in a soft fur coat. "Uncle Lang, you spoil me to death." She whirled toward him for another hug and only stopped to pose beside Carrol. "Look at us; as alike as two peas. You gave us watches alike last summer and now we have coats alike. Do we look alike?"

She tilted her brown head against Carrol's blond curls and danced on to snatch a shimmering pink evening frock from its tissue paper nest. "Dear Mummy," she said softly. "How do you suppose she ever managed to decide on it without me?"

The others laughed at her as she hovered joyously over their gifts, too. She was everywhere. She was as excited as the Parrishes always were over any event, large or small, and she made the Christmas gayer than any Houghton Christmas had ever been.

"When we were little," she said, when Mr. Houghton had gone to help his mother to her room and she and Carrol were arranging their gifts on tables, "we used to play store with our presents. Once David bought my doll and wouldn't give it back. Goodness, how I cried."

"Did he give it back?"

"Of course; he had to. But not until Daddy made him." She set a Christmas message from her family in a conspicuous place before an evening bag and pushed back her hair. "Golly, I'm hot," she said fanning herself. "Aren't you?"

"Nope." Carrol laid a vanity that bore the West Point crest back into its box, propped up its accompanying card that was engraved 'David Parrish' and nothing else, and stifled a hurt sigh. "You wouldn't be either," she said evenly, "if you'd take off that fur coat."

"Well, goodness, so I wouldn't." Penny caressed the soft beaver with her cheek and was slipping it off when Perkins surprised her with a letter.

"A special delivery just came for you, Miss Penny."

"Oh, grand! I'll bet it's from Dad. Thank you, Perkins."

Penny took the envelope, looked eagerly at the handwriting —and said in disgust: "Pooh! It's only from Louise."

"What do you suppose she wants?"

"I don't know. Shall we open it or save it for a dull moment?"

"We may as well read it and get the agony over."

They seated themselves on the floor in a littered paper setting and Penny grinned as she slit the flap. "If she wants to visit me again she's got another guess coming."

She drew out the letter, held it for Carrol to see, and they stared numbly at the first two lines.

"Dear Penny": (Louise had written).

"Isn't it terrible that David is blind!"

★

CHAPTER XI

David's Darkness

"I wish I could tell you that it isn't true—but I can't," Langdon Houghton said, leaning against the mantel and looking down at Penny, a small huddle in the corner of the divan. "We decided not to say anything to either one of you until we had something more definite to go on, one way or the other." His eyes met those of Carrol, saw their wide terror as they moved about the room, and he sighed. She feels it even more deeply than Penny does, he thought, his heart tight. She realizes what it means to *see*.

"What did Daddy say when he called you?" Penny brushed away her tears. "Is David frightened?"

"No, dear. He said that David was quite calm, and very brave, and sure that he will be all right. If David can keep from being frightened, Penny, the rest of us must carry on."

"I know it. Did he say how it happened?"

"In a way, yes. He said that David had been studying awfully hard for the Christmas writs. He was worried about them it seems, and he spent every spare minute that he had, working. He complained to Michael of headaches, but didn't say that his eyes bothered him."

"Did he just suddenly . . . ?"

"Michael says so. He said they were at their desks after the supper hour. David was reading history and Michael was so absorbed in something that at first he didn't hear what

115

David was saying. When he looked up David was turned to-ward him and was announcing, as calmly as though he were talking about the weather, 'Mike, I can't see my book, and I can't see you.' "

"What did they do?"

"They called the Tac right away and got David into the cadet hospital, then they called your father. I can't under-stand," Mr. Houghton frowned and rubbed his forehead, "how Louise would find out about it in time to have that wretched letter here so quickly. It's only been four days."

"I suppose Dick let it out, or somebody," Penny covered her face with her hands, then looked up through her tears. "I'll have to go home right away," she sobbed. "When could I go, Uncle Lang?"

"This afternoon, Penny. I'm going to let you talk to your mother and then I'm going to put you on a plane. You will be in New York this evening, and tomorrow you can see David. Come on, honey, we'll put in the call."

He drew her to her feet, his heart aching for her and for his own child who had left her chair to lift a compact from a circle of gifts. I can comfort Penny, he thought, as she clung to him, but what can I say to this still daughter of mine? I know what she feels because we're so alike—but what can I say to her?

He placed the call, and while Penny waited with the re-ceiver to her ear, crossed the room again. "Don't worry, dear," he said gently. "David will be all right."

"I know he will." Carrol looked down at the little box she held. "It's just . . ." she clutched the compact tighter, whis-pered, "I'll be back in a few minutes," and fled up the stairs.

As her door closed behind her she leaned against it, her breath coming in short gasps. "Oh, David, David," she sobbed, "I can't bear it." She flung herself on the bed, crying into the pillows until her throat ached. "It isn't fair," she moaned over and over. "I doubted you. I doubted your pitiful, scrawled

letter, and the card in my Christmas gift. I pretended I didn't
—but I did." She drew the compact from under her cheek
and caressed it. "You saw this," she whispered. "I know you
selected it yourself. And when it was time to send it, you
couldn't write the card."

For a long time she lay still, her mind going from David
in his darkness to Marjorie Parrish who had wrapped his gift,
tucking the bit of pasteboard inside; who had wrapped all the
gifts, making them beautiful and gay, and sending her love
and hope for happiness with them. She has courage, Carrol
thought, real courage.

Sternly, she forced herself to get up from the bed, to wash
her face and comb her hair, and to go resolutely down the
stairs. "Have you had your call, Penny?" she asked quietly
from the door.

"Yes." Penny went to meet her, her face brighter.
"Mummy said the headaches have stopped and that the doctors say the cause is functional instead of organic. I don't know
what that means but Uncle Lang says it's good."

"Is it, really, Daddy?" Carrol put her arm around Penny
and they went out to the porch where her father sat. "Does
it mean that things aren't hopeless?"

"It makes me feel a million years younger." He smiled re-
assuringly at them and went on to explain: "It means that no
organ of the eye is injured. The eyes are only tired from over-
strain; just as one's body collapses from too much labor."

"Then after he rests a while, he'll be all right?"

"I hope—and I think so, Penny."

He smiled at her and nodded but, as soon as she had gone
with Carrol to pack her Christmas things, he went into his
study and telephoned again. "What about a specialist from
New York, Dave?" he asked when Major Parrish was on the
wire. "You're sure? We don't want to leave a stone unturned.
All right. Call me tonight when Penny gets safely home, will
you? I'll be up the first of the week."

"I wish you were going with me," Penny said to Carrol as she laid an armload of gifts on the bed.

"I do, too." Carrol walked to the window and looked out at the green ocean rolling against the sand. Her mind seemed to have exploded, and small thoughts shot out like jagged fragments from a speeding comet. "There's a little wave trying to catch up with a big one," she remarked irrelevantly. "Are you going to wear your new coat?"

"I guess so." Penny laid the coat on a chair and went to stand beside Carrol. "You sound funny," she said unhappily. "I mean funny peculiar, not funny ha-ha. I hate to go away knowing that you're lonesome. I'd stay if it weren't that I can be a help to Mummy—with the children, and all."

"I know it, Pen." Carrol's voice was cheerful. "I want you to go. I only wish I could go with you."

"*Can't* you?"

"No." Carrol looked out at the ocean again. "It's strange," she said absently, as she twisted the cord of the Venetian blind, "that when one's upset, instead of suffering over a thing as a whole, little thoughts keep popping up. I find myself thinking of the beach towel we left down there and wondering if your laundry came back—and then, right in the midst of it there's a stab like a knife, and I remember the way David wears his cap."

"It's nature's way of taking care of us, I guess. If we thought too much and too long we'd go to pieces." Penny sighed and turned from the window to her collection on the bed. "I'm not much interested in these," she said as she fingered the evening gown that spilled its soft folds onto the floor. "That's funny peculiar, too."

"You will be." Carrol dropped the cord and squared her shoulders. "Someday, we'll look back on this as a bad dream. You sort out your things while I write David a note. I want you to read it to him privately. Will you?"

"Of course, darling! And it's going to buck him up no end."

Penny answered the challenge to courage with as brave a smile as she could manage, and Carrol went into her sitting room and to her desk. She stared at the white paper some time before her pen touched the sheet, but when she began to write she was unconscious of Penny's chatter with the maid who was helping her pack.

"David dear": she began.

"Before Penny reads you this she will have told you all the things I'm going to write, because she knows how much I am thinking of you. I'm so glad you are brave about it, David; nothing matters but that. That and the fact that you are going to come through this bad time . . ." she stopped and pressed her fingers to her eyes. *If I could only write the word, safely,* she thought. She looked at the blurred ink through her tears, then rubbed her eyes and substituted— "gallantly."

Her pen hurried on and on, for it was easier now. Christmas. Her compact. Telling of the things that she and Penny did, the silly nothings that they talked about; and ending with the hope that some way, somehow, she could come north soon.

When she finished, the bedroom was empty and she could hear Penny's voice in Madam Houghton's room, so she tucked the note into Penny's open dressing case and roamed restlessly through the house. The Christmas tree still blazed in forgotten splendor, so she switched off the lights. She opened the windows wide to soft sunshine and pushed the chairs back into their accustomed places. Idly she picked up Louise's letter from the floor where Penny had dropped it and glanced at the post-mark. West Point. Louise was at West Point. Louise was there to read to David; to chat with him; to cheer him up with bits of news and gossip. Louise was *there.*

Grimly she pressed her lips together. "It doesn't matter," she told herself above the pounding of her heart. "It doesn't matter what she does. I won't be jealous. I know David—I do. And if she can help him, even a little . . ." She tossed the letter into the empty fireplace and touched a match to it. "There. That for you," she told it as flames licked through the flourishing script. "You were mean enough to write to us when the Parrishes didn't want us to know, so you can't hurt us any more than you have." She was looking down at the ashes when Penny came in.

"Lunch," Penny said simply. "The cook wanted to rustle up some of the Christmas dinner for this noon but I told her we couldn't eat it. I'm all ready to go."

"Pen." Carrol knelt on the divan and looked at Penny imploringly. "Don't worry David with things when you go to see him. Forget all our other talks and just think of David. No matter what happens—don't give your feelings away. Promise?"

"Sure, but . . . I don't know what you mean."

"You will when you get there." Carrol thought of Louise, who would, no doubt, be very much in evidence, and added, "Just keep him happy. Now, let's call Daddy to lunch."

When Parker had driven a quiet, but outwardly cheerful trio to the airport, Penny stood looking up at the big plane that was to carry her home. It had none of the magic it would have held even one short day ago. Then she would have thought of it as a silver-winged bird; now it sat solidly on the ground, ponderous and powerful. Busses were disgorging passengers from the resort hotels; luggage was weighed; seats checked; and at the foot of the plane's moveable steps she held tightly to Mr. Houghton's hand.

"You're not frightened, are you, Penny?" he asked, looking down at her anxiously.

"No." She shook her head and moistened her lips. "Not of the plane trip. It's just that I hate to let go of you until I can clutch onto Mummy and Daddy. You've been so wonderful."

"Penny," he bent down and spoke to her soothingly,

"you've always been the one who managed things. Aren't you going to manage now, for David?"

"Yes, I am." Her head came up and her chin thrust forward, small and round and determined. "It's the waiting that's so hard."

"We know it is, Penny, because Daddy and I have to go on waiting." Carrol looked longingly at the plane. "You're going *home*. Keep thinking of that."

"I will." Penny kissed them quickly, clung to each for a second, then hurried up the steps.

It's queer, she thought, looking out at the clouds, I'm not even interested in the people around me. Once I would have wondered if the little old lady across from me is going to see her grandchildren, and would have told her all about Bobby and Tippy. Now I don't care. She leaned back wearily, and the stewardess, who was young and pretty, looked admiringly at the beaver coat flung carelessly over the chair back; at the brown curls spraying out over it; at the small, tired face staring out of the window.

"Do you feel ill?" she asked, bending over. "Is there anything I can do for you?"

"No, thank you." Penny's smile was sweet but fleeting. She huddled deeper into her chair and closed her eyes to hide the ache in them, and the hostess turned away.

She's a queer child, she thought. Probably has rich parents who don't want her with them.

She speculated about Penny during the long afternoon and, as she took away an untouched dinner tray, was sure that a lonely Christmas was responsible for a loss of appetite. But when the plane glided onto La Guardia Field, when the passengers were helped down, and Penny was held in the embrace of a woman so like her that she could only be her mother, the young hostess glanced at them and shrugged.

"Probably just spoiled," she decided, smiling at the little old lady who was waving to a group of children inside the entrance gates. "Probably mad because she had to come back from Florida."

"Oh, Mummy," Penny was saying, "is David any better?"

"He says he feels fine now. He's still wearing the bandages so we don't know about his eyes." She released Penny and looked at the array of bags waiting to be claimed. "Did you bring *all* your luggage on the plane, darling?"

"Umhum. It must have cost an awful lot on excess but Uncle Lang insisted that I'd feel better if I had my Christmas with me. Where's Daddy?"

"He waited with the car so he could bring it around quickly. We want to drive back as soon as we can." She patted Penny's sober face and smiled her sweet, warm smile. "You're brown as a berry, aren't you? And I see you have on your beautiful coat I helped select. Isn't Uncle Lang a darling?"

"Oh, Mummy, he's wonderful." Some of the misery left Penny's face as she met her mother's interested look. And at her father's "Hello, baby. Gosh, it's good to have you back!" she climbed in between them and laid a hand on each knee. They felt warm and strong and comforting. Just like always, she thought, making an effort to entertain them with descriptions of the Houghton cottage and all that she and Carrol had done.

When they spoke of David they were as casual as when they spoke of the little children, and once Major Parrish said, "It was a darn shame he couldn't have had Christmas at home, but we made quite an occasion of it in his room. Some of the boys from the ward came in for a minute."

"And he loved the super-special sun glasses you sent him," her mother said with a pleased nod. "He put them on over the bandages and looked so silly. They'll be grand for him when gets out and about."

"Yes, they will." Penny gulped and wished for the hundredth time that she had chosen anything but glasses for

David. "There's so little you can get for a cadet," she explained haltingly. "And I didn't know. . . ."

"You couldn't have found anything better." They were winding through the hills now and, sensing her embarrassment at the inappropriate gift, her father patted her knee. "Don't you worry about David," he said with pride in his voice. "He's every inch a soldier."

And when she saw him, Penny knew he was. She had walked slowly along the corridor, dreading the feel of the doorknob under her hand; but when she reached it the door was open and David was calling,

"Well, come on in, Penny. I hear you clumping along. Had a good vacation?"

"Hello, David." Penny was thankful he couldn't see her tears. She blinked them back and said with a sob she tried to turn into a chuckle, "Perfect. You're having a little vacation, yourself."

His face was turned toward her and the grin that crinkled his cheeks over the bandage was wide. He looked very long in the iron bed and his slender, sensitive hands were brown on the white coverlid. He lifted one in a gesture of salute and Penny was grateful that he didn't grope toward her.

"Thanks for the specs. I'm going to need 'em."

"I hope . . ." Penny caught the "so" before it reached her lips, and added breathlessly, "that it won't be long until you do."

"Any day now."

A nurse came in the door, starched and rustling, and David's grin was still there as he greeted her gruffly. "Here *you* come again. Every time I get a pretty girl in here, you crackle in and out."

"I'm pretty, too," the nurse retorted. "You're going to be sorry for all the mean things you've said to me. When they take off your blinders you'll get a view of my flaming beauty that will stagger you." She was plain, forty and competent, and she winked at Penny as she turned back an edge of the gauze to pour liquid on the pads beneath.

"You drip on me." David wiped a drop from his nose and reached toward her. "Hold my hand," he coaxed. "You never want to stick around and hold my hand."

"I never have time. You cadets keep me too busy waiting on you." She smoothed the pillows and her fingers hovered over the shining, rumpled curls. "Be a good boy, now, and don't bounce around." She smiled down at him again, nodded to Penny, and rustled out.

"The boys call her 'old Horse Teeth,'" David said when he was sure she had gone, "but she's a swell old gal." He turned his head toward Penny. "Bring your chair over here and tell me about Carrol. Was she—was she upset about my little bust-up?"

Penny needed no second invitation. She dragged her chair to his bed, propped her feet on its iron side rail, and launched with fervor into a recital of her southern trip. Her heart felt lighter now that she had seen David. She could meet his gaiety and courage with a matching sparkle; and she was near bursting when, after she had read Carrol's letter, he said,

"I wish you'd let me dictate one to her, Pen. I've thought about it every day but there hasn't been anyone who understands enough for me to say the things I want to say. Boy, I'm glad you're home."

"Oh, Davy, I am, too." She leaned over impulsively to hug him, and felt like Clara Barton and the whole Red Cross as she rushed to bring the scratch pad and pencil she had hopefully brought in her purse.

He makes me feel confident, she thought as, pencil poised, she waited for him to begin.

"Carrol darling": David dictated, then stopped and grinned. "I know you're wide-eyed and all aflutter over the salutation," he said, "but it doesn't mean a thing. So write it down and stop wiggling."

"I wrote it down and I'm not wiggling." Penny was prim. "It looks to me as if you're the self-conscious one."

"Well, maybe I am, but it's a heck of a mess when a fellow has to let a prying sister know everything he says to another girl." He drew his knees up and clasped his hands around them. "Darn it," he muttered, "I can't do this."

"Oh, yes you can, Davy. Look." Penny reached over to pat him. "Just pretend I'm a stenographer, and I won't cheep until you get through.

"Okay."

David began again and for almost a paragraph Penny contained her emotions, as well as her suggestions for slight alterations in a style she considered most unromantic. "Wait a minute," she interrupted when she could bear it no longer. "Instead of saying 'I miss you like heck' don't you think it would sound nicer to put 'if I could only have you here beside my bed'?"

"Gosh, no!" David's yell made her jump, and when he flung his legs flat again she dropped the pad she had propped against the bed. "Throw the darn letter away," he shouted.

"Now, David, don't get excited." Penny retrieved the pad and hurried to placate him. She planned to make a few alterations in the finished copy; and by soothing, coaxing and as a last resort, threatening him with a complete epistle of her own composition, got a framework that by careful remodeling, could be built into a magnificent structure.

An hour rushed by. With the letter safely stowed away in her purse, she was talking happily of Carrol when a soft voice in the door brought her head around.

"Hello, children. When did you get home, Pen?"

Penny's mouth fell open and she blinked. Louise stood in the door, a book under one arm, and bearing a cardboard container from which two straws protruded.

"I brought the usual malted milk, Davy," she continued,

pitching the book on the bed and putting David's fingers around the container. "How goes it today?"

She looked down at him, her eyelashes sweeping her cheek, her black hair a dusky cloud on her coat and her lips smiling possessively. "I got the English Lit book we need."

"Thanks." David took a pull from one straw and Louise leaned down to sip from the other.

"Ummm. Not bad today." She turned away to slip off her coat and said over her shoulder to Penny: "How was the trip?"

"Fair." Penny settled herself more firmly in the only chair. She was angry and puzzled and her thoughts were chaotic. Does she come every day? she wondered. Has she been here all the time, and who under the sun is she visiting?

David sensed her inarticulate dismay, for he held the malted milk toward her. "Want a swig?" he offered. "Louise has been staying with the Grahams because it was too far to go back to Arden for the holidays."

Penny shook her head, forgetting he couldn't see her, then gently pushed his hand away. "No, thanks."

"She sure has been swell about getting me a bit ahead with my reading." He turned his head to the corner where Louise was unfastening her goloshes. "How did you get hold of the book?"

"Through a brother plebe." Louise set her goloshes together, looked suggestively at Penny and the chair, and asked, "Do I sit, stand, or take to the floor for our session?"

"You'd better go now, Pen," David said quickly. "Visitors' hours won't last much longer."

"All right." Penny was hurt. She got up from the chair, took her new coat from the small closet and flung it on. "Any message for Mums?" she asked, shrugging away from Louise who was stroking the soft fur.

"Just tell her I'm fine. You'll come tomorrow?"

"I don't know. Maybe. At least some member of the family

will come." Penny stalked to the door, then her heart seemed to melt and she turned back. " 'By, Davy, dear," she said. "I'll be here."

"Fine. And Penny," David lifted himself on an elbow . . . "you won't forget the letter to Carrol, will you? It's pretty important to me."

"I'll mail it tonight." She flicked a glance at Louise and tossed off carelessly, "Good-by, teacher. Do I see you to-morrow, too?"

"Probably. I seem to have become indispensable." Louise sat down in the vacated chair and took the book from David. "Run along. You bother us."

Penny went through the halls muttering to herself. "I could murder her," she told a closed door. "She's always up-setting my life. And David, the dumb dodo, seems to have forgiven and forgotten." She thought of David as he had looked leaning on his elbow, his poor sightless face talking of Carrol. "I'd like to tell him how mean Louise was to write me that letter." Then she sighed. I'll bet Carrol figured out that Louise was here, she thought as she trudged off through the snow. Somehow she knew it, and that's why she warned me to do anything to keep David happy. I did a mighty poor job of it the first jolt I had.

Large flakes were drifting down in the gathering dusk as Penny tramped along, lost in her thoughts. She was halfway home and telling Louise to mind her own affairs when she stopped and looked around her.

"Heavens, I've left the car behind!" she cried. "I must be upset."

She turned around and ran back along the way she had come. Now and then she scuffled and slid, leaving sweeping tracks behind her, her eyes on David's window where a light blazed out onto the white world. "I want you to see it, David," she whispered across the dusk, "and I'm so afraid you never will."

★

CHAPTER XII

FOUR IN A WARD

"We used to be the happy Parrishes," Penny complained to Trudy as she looked out disconsolately at the snow-laden trees, "and now look at us."

"You're still the happy Parrishes," Trudy answered tartly. "At least your mama and your papa is. You'd be, too, if you'd stop worryin' about Miss Louise and her monkeyshines."

"But it isn't just Louise, Trudy." Penny left the window to take one corner of the sheet Trudy was unfolding. "It's thinking about David all the time. You talk as if Mums and Dad aren't nearly crazy with worry."

" 'Course they is." Trudy tucked the sheet in snugly and reached for a blanket. "But they don't go around a-sighin' and a-huntin' up more troubles than they's got."

"But what if David never sees again?"

"He'll see. If Mr. David never sees with his eyes, he'll see with his ears an' his hands an' his heart. Life ain't goin' to whip Mr. David." She finished making the bed and turned to pick up a small pair of bedroom slippers. "I've known him since he wore shoes smaller than these," she added, looking down at Tippy's wooly slippers. "He's always walked straight. Even when he was learnin' to walk he knew where he was goin', an' he went there. I ain't worryin' about him, an' I ain't worryin' about your mama nor your papa." She set the slippers on a closet shelf and looked obliquely at Penny.

"You're worrying about me?"

"No, I'm not worryin' about you, neither; not when you stop your play-actin'. The trouble with you is you got a heart that's too big for your body. But you gotta learn to manage it. Your heart says 'I'm mighty unhappy. Let's don't eat.' So you don't eat. Then the rest of you gets all out of fix. Your mind cain't work right, no more than a car can run without gasoline. Your nerves is a-jumpin'—an' first thing you know, your heart's runnin' everything an' your body jes' sets down an' quits. You mustn't let that happen, honey."

"I know it." Penny burrowed her head into Trudy's shoulder. "I've always thought I was the steady member of the family, but perhaps I've got too dramatic this winter. Mummy has always seemed to be the excitable one, but when it comes to real courage, she's ready."

"You is, too." Trudy, satisfied with her little lecture, shook Penny loose and suggested, "How about me fixin' you a little breakfast? Some nice eggs an' bacon an' toast?"

"All right." Penny followed along the hall and when they reached the kitchen, sat on the table watching Trudy at the stove. "You know," she confided as she put a slice of bread in the toaster, "ever since I saw Miss Ware and met some actors I've had the idea that I'm going to set the world on fire."

"You can. I told you Mr. David always walks straight. You can, too, if you quit this back-trackin' an' jumpin around."

"But I haven't the right even to think of it now." Penny's eyes were big as she looked at Trudy. "You said, yourself . . ."

"Miss Penny." Trudy closed her own eyes. "Oh, Lord," she prayed, "give this child some sense. I ain't askin' anything for Mr. David, 'cause you're takin' care of him. But this other child of mine. . . ." She was silent for some seconds, then she said, "Thank you, Lord," and took Penny her bacon and eggs.

Penny looked down at the plate and her lips quivered. "I needed just that, I guess," she said unsteadily. "Maybe now I've grown up."

"Maybe. But I doubts it." Trudy grinned as she saw Penny settled in a corner of the breakfast room with her tray. "Up to now you been broke out with trouble like it was the measles, an' your face looked like it was a quarantine sign that was a-tellin' folks to keep away from you. That ain't good, honey."

"I know it." Penny gulped her breakfast, eagerly planning what she would do for David.

She tapped along the corridor that afternoon, practising a gay greeting should Louise have arrived before her; but when she opened the door the room was empty. A piece of notepaper on the stiffly made bed bore a straggling message and she picked it up.

"Am in the ward with the other fellows. Hooray!" David had printed.

Penny dropped the note and sprinted down the hall. At the second closed door she paused, patted the "beany" on the back of her head, smoothed the curls cascading from under it and inspected the seams of her stockings. She knocked timidly and at the voice that called, "Come in if you're young and beautiful," turned the knob.

Four cadets occupied beds. Two, like David, were tucked neatly under their covers, but the fourth in his gray West Point bathrobe was sitting on the spread, using his pillow for a table while he played solitaire.

"Well, hello," he welcomed, throwing down his cards. "Here's your little sister, Blinker. Come in and see us," he invited, as Penny hesitated in the door. "We won't bite you."

"Hi, Pen." David pushed himself higher on his pillows. "That's Jones, W.R., doing all the bawling. He's captain of the football team and known as Jonesy. Martin Cromwell, here on my left; and Jack Barton over there in the corner somewhere. I'm hobnobbing with the top crust, now."

"That's fine. Hello." Penny closed the door and stood uncertainly just inside; but Jones, W.R., swung himself from his high bed and dragged a chair across the floor.

"Where would you choose to sit?" he asked. "Over there by Blinker, or out in the middle where we all can see you,— or over here by me?"

"I'll sit by David."

"Okay. But he gets all the girls."

He set her chair in place and returned to his own cot where he sat cross-legged, staring at her. The other two bolstered up their pillows for a better view, and Penny looked around at the battery of eyes.

"Go on and talk to Blink," Jack Barton said from his corner. "Don't mind us; we like to listen."

Penny, searching for something to say, looked at David. He was plumping up his pillows, too, and she would have helped him but for a warning shake of the head from the next bed. "Why do they call you Blinker?" she asked when David was settled.

"They say I'm like one of those blinker lights at street crossings. They go on and off, and just now, I'm off."

"It's cute." She grinned and the other three regarded her solemnly.

"Any news from home?"

"Nothing new. Trudy gave me the dickens this morning."

"She did?" David chuckled. "I'm expecting her over here any day to light into me."

"Who's Trudy?" The voice came from the far corner as cadet Barton sat up straighter. "Do we know her?"

"She's our cook." Penny laughed at his disappointment. "She bakes cakes and pies."

"Don't tell me about it." He fell back with a groan and Penny tapped a tin box on her lap.

"She sent one to David."

"No fooling?" Jonesy uncoiled himself again and leaped over to help Penny pull off the lid. "We've been waiting for boodle, and this looks . . ." he tugged at the lid and smacked his lips as it lifted . . . "what I call *good!*"

"My knife's over there," Jack said, pointing to the dresser. "Cut her in thirds and don't cheat on me."

"But what about David?" Penny reached for the cake that was already halfway across the room. "It's *his* cake; doesn't he get any?"

"Plebes don't rate cake. He can have whatever we don't eat."

"Well, of all things!" Penny looked at David but he was grinning.

"When my sister comes back from the Post Exchange," he predicted, "and brings two malted milks, you're going to be sorry."

"We'll give you a piece of cake, Blinker. We'll give you a nice big piece." Jonesy was cutting the cake in fifths.

"Sure, Blinker; we were only kidding."

"You can even have part of my piece for a malted milk."

Penny looked at them, one at a time, and reached for her coat. "Here I go, out into the cold," she groaned. "Malted milks it is."

She skipped along the hall, happy because David was so happy, and grateful to the teasing boys. When she returned, laden with paper sacks, another voice was booming in the room and a strange cadet was the center of attention on her chair.

"This is Mr. Stevenson," Jonesy said to her as he took the sacks. "Miss Parrish, you are now meeting the greatest football player the corps has ever had—and the dumbest student. He not only had enough skins to take up his whole Christmas furlough, but he may be here until he's an old man."

Cadet Stevenson stood up to shake hands with Penny, and

Jonesy removed his chair. He returned it to David's bed, took the glass that held a toothbrush, and stretched the five malted milks to six. "Here's to us guys so dumb we couldn't go home for the holidays," he toasted, holding his glass aloft, "and to one plebe who couldn't have gone home anyway. Blink, I'll set your cake on your chest. Don't goop."

David groped for the glass on his night table, took a swallow and carefully put it back again while Jonesy stood watching him. He was fumbling for the thick wedge of devil's food that nestled in a towel on his chest, when Jonesy's hand forestalled him.

"Ah-ah," he warned. "Don't touch it. We forgot your vitamins."

"Now listen!" David growled and pushed the hand away. "I'm full of vitamins from A to Z. Give me a break, can't you?"

"Well, maybe. Once." Jonesy straightened the towel and picked up his own drink. "But don't blame me if you can only see out of one eye."

I'm happy, happy, happy, Penny thought as she listened or joined the talk. "David's better—he *looks* better—and Louise could walk in now and I wouldn't mind."

As though she had evoked her presence, Louise did walk in, precisely at that moment. She greeted the football hero with a casual "Hi, Steve," and acknowledged the introductions as informally as they were made. She was assured and very beautiful in the clear afternoon sunlight and, Penny, hooking her feet firmly around the rungs of her chair, thought —quite aware of it.

"Sorry we ate all the boodle," Jonesy said as he munched his cake. "You should have come earlier."

"So I see." Louise leaned over to take a bite from the piece Penny offered and went on to David. "Hi, Butch," she greeted, looking down at him. "I see you're wearing brown polka dots this season."

"Darned crumbs." David wadded up the towel and dusted the cake from his chest to the floor. "You're late, teacher."

"It's my public. All the cadets left over for Christmas suddenly discovered my charms." She accepted a chair from Jonesy with a casual thanks and reached for the book on the table.

"Not today," Jack Barton called from his bed across the room. "This is a party in celebration of Blinker's release from confinement, and I'll be darned if we'll listen to Oklahoma's joining the Union."

"O-kay." Louise slapped the book back on the table and posed with an arm resting on David's bed. "I'd rather fascinate five men with my beauty than my brains, anyway."

"What brains? And I might add, what beauty?" Cadet Stevenson peered at her quizzically. "Or was that what knocked Blinker blind?"

"Oh, he never saw me. To Blinker, if that's what you call him now, I'm just the home town gal who hasn't made good. Am I right, David?"

"Well, you're rapidly living down your past." David smiled under his bandages and Louise patted his hand.

There was an undercurrent to their conversation that Penny disliked. Her eyebrows drew together like magnetized wickets, but she jerked them back. Trudy's warning that her face was a placard, either to isolate or include her, erased her scowl and she was surprised at the apparent ease with which she could control her emotions. Just acting, she thought as she turned to talk to Martin Cromwell.

Compared with Louise's pert assurance, her naive remarks and unstudied wit amused the room so much that Cromwell forgot his recently removed appendix, Barton ceased to mind the cast that held his leg, and Jonesy dismissed whatever minor aches and pains he had concocted for his rest cure. The nurse bustled in, soaked the pads on David's eyes, grumbled and growled and grinned at them, and bustled out again.

"Poor old Horse Teeth. I'd take her to the dance tonight if I weren't laid up," Jonesy said. "Her life's just one dull spot followed by another duller one. *Now* who's knocking?" He got down from his bed, shouted the usual "Come in if you're young and beautiful," and went to the door.

When it opened, his burly figure blocked it, and Penny, the ever-curious, leaned over to peer around him and to gasp. "Carrol!" she squealed. "How under the sun did you get here?"

Her chair went over with a crash, the bedridden patients raised up for a better view, and Louise's mouth stayed where an unfinished word had left it.

"I came up with Daddy." Carrol smiled at everyone and, dragging Penny behind her like a small anchor, hurried across the room to David. "Hello, Louise. Hello, David. You don't look sick."

"I'm not." David's hands reached out to hold hers tightly. "I'll be out of here in a few days. Gee, it's swell to see you."

Carrol knew that he was seeing her. "Same cute little hat that matches your coat," he said, rubbing his fingers along the squirrel of her sleeve. "Blue dress?"

"Umhum."

"Gosh." He turned her toward the room, introduced an admiring audience that stared from its beds like three bears grinning at Goldilocks, and added: "Remember my blindness, fellows, and give me a break."

"Sure. Just relax." Steve, the athlete hero, stepped forward to extend an impressive hand to Carrol, and Jonesy removed his chair again.

"Sit right here, Carrol," he invited, setting the chair close to his own bed. "Blinker's already surrounded."

"She can have my place." Louise swished to the center of the room, accepted the circulating chair that Steve was retrieving for himself, and sat herself down. "I have to leave in a minute."

"Why?" Penny turned from Carrol and a flood of eager questions. "Visiting hours aren't up yet."

"I know it, darling; I can still tell time." Louise held up a wrist that displayed a minute watch glittering ostentatiously in diamonds. "I happen to have a date."

"Dick?"

"No, not Dick. A first classman." She tried to look nonchalant but the words had a pleasant sound and the temptation to add to them was too great. "He's a lieutenant in M Company."

"Hot dawg." Jonesy straddled his bed and leaned his chin on the foot of it. "Imagine a cadet lieutenant having to strut around here through the holidays with only a bunch of plebes and nit-wits to look at him. This is probably his big moment, girl, and you'd better not keep him waiting."

"I won't." Louise turned to Carrol. "Are you home for good?"

"No, just for a week. My father had to come up on business and he brought me with him." Carrol looked at Penny. "You don't know it yet," she told her, "but you have a guest."

"Not really!" Joy washed over Penny's face in a sunlight trail. "Does Mums know?"

"Umhum. Daddy and I took my bags over. She sent you her love, David, and she and Daddy will be over this evening."

Conversation hovered around David's bed and Louise's elaborate arrangements for departure caused no flurry.

"Thanks, Louise," David called as she said a haughty good-by from the door: "Have fun."

"I always do." Steve followed her with a casual "I'll trot along with you," and she glanced back at the book on the table. She decided to leave it for another visit, then, as he held the door for her, came back and picked it up. "I'll take this with me," she said. "You won't be needing me tomorrow."

"Why not?" David asked in surprise. "I still have to catch up with my work."

"You have others to help you." She tucked the book under her arm, squeezed past Carrol, and gave them all a casual flick of a wave.

"But the book." David lifted himself from his pillows. "You've been a brick to help me, Louise, and I feel like a heel for having taken so much of your time—but, gosh, I can't do anything without that book."

"Sorry. Someone else can borrow one. I'm leaving the day after tomorrow, anyway. Good-by." She breezed through the door and David fell back.

"Sweet child, isn't she?" Jonesy remarked. "What stirred her up?"

"I did, I'm afraid." Carrol looked apologetically at David. "I'm sorry, David, but I'll get a book and read to you."

"Oh, Blink doesn't mind, do you Blink?" Penny grinned, relieved that Louise was once again removed from her world; then she pointed to David. "That's his new name. Cute, isn't it?"

The name was explained again, this time by Jonesy, and David said when he had finished, "You know, I really am blinking back here behind this mess of cotton." He explored the bandage with his fingers. "And I'll bet I could see as well as I ever did if they'd take the darn stuff off."

"I know you could." Carrol leaned forward. "Have you any idea when they're going to do it?"

"Tomorrow or the next day. Boy, I'll be glad to look on the world again."

Silence answered him. Five pairs of eyes that could see looked at his smiling confidence, and most of them held pity —and all of them held fear.

"It—it will be wonderful," Carrol managed.

"Of course it will only be for a second or two at first, but . . ." He reached toward her and she put her hand in his. "I'd like to have you here if they'll let you come. Mums and Dad can tell you when it's to be."

"I'll be here, Davey. If I can't be inside, I'll be in the hall. You know," she leaned across him and put Penny's hand in David's, too, "I came all the way from Florida just to be with you and Pen."

"I thought you'd come. Somehow, I knew that some afternoon you'd come walking in." He covered the two small hands with his big one. "I didn't want either one of you to know because it would spoil your holiday, but after you found out—gosh, I was glad."

"We were, too." Penny released herself and stood up. "I'll gather up my stuff because it's almost time to go."

Jonesy winked at her, patted his heart, and coming to help her with her box and the empty cartons, said with a simper: "Ain't love grand?" He scowled at his curious and staring roommates until they slid down into their covers, then he said to Penny, "They haven't any manners."

With a few sweeps he cleaned the room, replaced the chair that had had a wandering afternoon and helped Penny with her coat. "Time's up," he said as he shook her down into it very much as he would blanket a football player after a hard-fought game. "Old pickle-puss will be along with the trays."

"We're off. Come Carrol, my pet." Penny snatched up her box and shook David's feet under the covers. "Be a good boy."

"I'll try." David gave Carrol's fingers a squeeze and released them reluctantly.

"Tomorrow, David," she said softly. "We'll hover around until they let us in."

"We'll still be here, too," Jack Barton reminded from his corner. "So you might bring some more boodle."

"What do you want?" Penny stopped in the door to ask.

"Pie." David suggested. "Tell Trudy to send some cookies and a mince pie."

"All right, but it's a funny mixture."

They waved, stepped back to admit an orderly with the first supper tray, and Carrol, as she closed the door, had a glimpse of David fumbling with his dishes. "What do you really think, Penny?"

"We don't know for sure." Penny shook her head. "But the doctors say the chances are ten to one that the rest will have done the trick. It's that one chance that keeps us in suspense; and they have a lot of fancy names for the reason that it sometimes happens."

"I wish tomorrow were over," Carrol sighed as they went out into the icy air. "Have you your car?"

"Umhum."

"Then we'll go in a caravan. I'll follow you."

They drove away and once more Penny looked up at the lighted windows. But this time she smiled.

CHAPTER XIII

DINNER FOR EIGHT

Carrol and Penny were awake early the next morning. They hurried into their clothes and ran downstairs to find Major and Mrs. Parrish already finishing their breakfast.

"Are they going to take off David's bandages this morning?" Penny asked as she slid into her place at the table.

"Yes, Colonel Pearson called me a few minutes ago." Major Parrish lifted his eyebrows and shook his head toward Bobby and Tippy. "Did you sleep well?" he asked Carrol.

"Like a top. It's so good to be back in my own bed." Carrol hugged Tippy and retied the bib that was slipping from under her fat little chin. "Are you glad to see me, Tippy?"

"Yes, I am." Tippy leaned forward to look at Carrol. "Did you know David's sick?" she asked in a hushed voice. "He's awfully sick."

"He's blind." Bobby's head wagged up and down impressively. "He can't see beans."

"Oh, dear." Mrs. Parrish looked at them and then at her husband. "How do you suppose they heard that, Dave?" she sighed. "We've been so careful not to talk about it."

"From other chidren, I suppose." He pulled Bobby's hand from the sugar bowl where it was groping, as Bobby, eyes tightly shuttered, was endeavoring to prepare his cereal. "Stop being silly."

"I was just seeing how it would feel to be like David. I don't like it."

"Well, David wouldn't like it either if he had to stay that way, but he doesn't, so get on with your meal." Major Parrish sounded gruff but the others saw the pain on his face and Penny threw herself into the breach.

"Could I drive you over to the horse-pistol in my car?" she asked. "Carrol and I thought we'd wander over this morning."

"We'd better take two cars because I have to go on to work." He glared at Bobby who was sanguinely stirring his oatmeal, his curly head bent over the bowl preparatory for connection with a dripping spoon. "You're a nuisance," he said fondly. "See if you can keep out of mischief this morning."

"We will, Daddy." Tippy's eyes that were the blue of a rain-washed sky looked up at him. "We'll be extra good today." She reached up for her mother's kiss and went solemnly on with her meal.

Colonel Pearson was making his rounds when the Parrishes and Carrol gathered in his office, so they went on up the stairs. Voices came from the only cadet ward in use during the holidays and Major Parrish opened the door while the others waited behind him. He looked into the room and Penny caught his sleeve.

"Could we come in, too, Daddy?" she whispered.

"I'll find out." He went inside and in a few minutes came out with the doctor.

Colonel Pearson wore a white surgical gown over his uniform, and after he had greeted them with a brusque good morning he said to Mrs. Parrish, "I know you are very anxious, and it's quite natural that you should want to be with your son. It's impossible for the girls, however . . ." he scowled at Carrol and Penny, tense and hopeful, then relented . . . "perhaps if they slip in very quietly. . . ."

"Oh, Colonel Pearson," Penny breathed, "we will. We'll sit clear across the room."

"Very well. But it must be understood that David is to think this merely a matter of routine. He isn't to know that anyone but his father is in the room. We have every confidence, of course, but should he not see, it might upset him."

"We understand, Colonel Pearson," Mrs. Parrish said gratefully. "Thank you for letting us come in."

He turned abruptly away, re-entered the room and, when they heard him talking with his nurse and David, they slipped through the door.

"Hi," Jonesy mouthed silently while Martin Cromwell clasped his hands together in a good-luck handshake and Jack Barton offered Mrs. Parrish a corner of his bed to sit on. They were watching the doctor as he unwound the layers of gauze and Major Parrish walked lightly across the room.

"Hello, son," he greeted David from over Colonel Pearson's shoulder. "Everything under control this morning?"

"Everything's fine," David answered. "I'll have a look at you in a minute." He was sitting up, hands relaxed around his knees and his head lifted under the deft fingers.

"All ready, now. Here go the pads." The colonel handed the last of the gauze to the waiting nurse and spoke quietly. "Take it easy and don't strain. Give your eyes time to become adjusted to the light before you try to focus on any object. Ready?"

"Ready."

He lifted off the cotton and stood holding it, looking down over his glasses.

When the pressure was relieved, David opened his eyes slowly. His small audience leaned forward and Penny's hand flew to her mouth when he closed them again. He blinked a few times, rapidly, then slowly and carefully, and looked toward the doctor and his father.

"Hi, Dad," he grinned. "I told you I'd see you. Kind of fuzzy yet, but you're there—and getting clearer."

"You bet I'm here."

Major Parrish was beside the bed, David's hand in his. His mother was there, too.

"It's swell, Mums." David took her hand on his other side, then his eyes reached across the room to Carrol. Before she could answer his smile the pads were on again.

"All right, Miss Green," Colonel Pearson's voice clipped out. "Give me the drops and then the eye-shade and dark glasses."

"You mean . . ." David's voice shook with excitement, "you mean I'm going to see—all *day*?"

"Of course you're going to see. You're going to get up and walk around and take life easy. You can wait on the sick ones now, but you're not to read or play cards with young Jones over there."

"Gosh, that's swell!" David submitted to the drops and

made jokes with the other cadets while the shade and glasses were fitted on.

"You look like a bug, David," Penny said when the doctor and Major Parrish had gone, "a pop-eyed bug."

"I don't care whether I'm pop-eyed or cross-eyed. I can see! And I'm tired of this darned bed. If you'll all go away for a minute I'll get some clothes on."

"I'm going grocery buying, anyway, darling," his mother answered, anticipating his desire to be on his feet and master of himself again. "And the girls can come back this afternoon." She leaned down to smile into the smoky lenses. "I'm so happy, David, and so grateful. Please be careful, dear."

"You can bet I will. I'll give my eyes such tender treatment they'll think they're a couple of star sapphires." He squinted at Carrol. "You'll be back—at two o'clock sharp?"

"We'll be back, but definitely."

"And don't forget the boodle." Jonesy tossed David his bathrobe and picked up his cards. "We'll be plenty hungry by then."

"I'll bet Trudy's baking now," Penny laughed. "She is if Dad telephoned her. But maybe we'd better run and do it so she won't worry. See you all later."

She hustled them out, the perfect manager again; and her mother was docile and satisfied to leave because she knew David's afternoon would be gay. Her own afternoon, with her sewing perhaps, and a view from her bedroom window of the beautiful world David could see, would be enough. So she blew him a kiss and followed Penny's skipping goloshes.

"Everything is practically perfect," Penny said half an hour later, dusting the snow from her mittens and stamping her feet at the side door. "I put my heart and soul into that snow fight. It made us feel grand. Funny how one week you can be swimming in the ocean and the next rolling in the snow."

Their cheeks were glowing, white flakes clung to their hair and their coats looked sugar-coated. They left white dots on the hall rug as they tracked to a note Trudy had pinned to a lamp, and dripped sparkles on the table when they bent over to read it.

"Have taken the children to town," Trudy had written. "New York called up."

"Now who could that be that 'called up'?" Penny wondered. "Do you think it was your father?"

"It might be, but I doubt it." Carrol shook her hair loose from her parka and flung off her coat. "Who else could it be?"

"I wouldn't know. But I'm curious." Penny pulled the telephone to her and asked for long distance. She chatted with the friendly operator who kept daily track of the post's affairs, and wrenched out a shuddering "Oh!" as she turned back to Carrol. "It's that dumb-dodo friend of yours, Denise," she said, her hand over the mouthpiece. "She's been calling every five minutes. I'll bet she wants to come up here. What shall I do?"

"Have her." The voice from above was her mother's and Penny looked upward in surprise.

"Greetings," she waved. "Where did you pop up from? I don't want her," she went on without waiting for an answer.

"That's why I say have her. In every letter you've written to her you've invited her. Have a house party if you need to. I'm so happy I don't care if the house overflows." Her mother went singing down the hall and Penny hunched her shoulders in despair.

Her call came through and she found herself exclaiming pleasantly at the prospect of a New Year's visit from not only Denise, but Faith as well, and promising glibly that dates would be on hand for a "bang-up bust."

"Now why did I do that!" she exclaimed. "I know Mums is tired and everyone is ready for a let-down."

Carrol laughed as she looked at Penny's grumpy face. "You

know you did it because you wanted to," she told her. "You know you could never resist excitement."

"Well, I have it, and David won't be here to help. Oh, dear." She clumped up the stairs and stood in her mother's door, hands on hips. "Now see what you've done," she scolded. "You got me into a mess of trouble."

"Make out a list for a dinner party for New Year's Eve," her mother said happily. "Just the eight of you. In the afternoon you can all be with David, and it will be good for him."

"Okay." Penny bounced across the room and coddled her mother's head in her arms. "Dear, grand little Mums," she whispered, with no regard for her mother's nose that was crushed against her. "Sometime we're going to stop and think about you."

"When that day comes I'll be too old to enjoy it—I hope," Majorie Parrish answered, freeing herself. "Can you find dates for everyone on such short notice?"

"Sure. I've got one with Michael, and Carrol can drag Dick, and David can think up a couple of other boys. Maybe it's going to be fun."

Penny whistled her way back to Carrol and they spent the rest of the morning in the guest room making plans and beds. In the afternoon David's assistance in the matter of dates was unnecessary as Jonesy, to be discharged from the hospital "in perfect physical health," could find no further excuse for his rest cure and comfort. "I'll drag the best-looking one," he offered generously, "and we'll get Steve to give the other one a whirl. That ought to thrill 'em."

"Oh, dear." Penny sat down with a thump. "You mean one of those out of town dubs is going with a first classman and one with the captain of the team—and both of them with football players? That's not fair."

"I know it, but there's only one of me—and you've got a date. I'd rather take Carrol but I'm scared of Blinker." Jonesy smirked at Carrol and besought David archly. "Could

I take Carrol? I'd be awful careful of her and I'd try my best not to beat your time."

"I'll bet you would." David, cross-legged on his bed smiled at Carrol. "Go ahead," he said, "if you think you can do it."

"You might try; others have and failed." Carrol's dimple flashed out before she turned her head from David. "We'll give Dick and Steve to the absent ones," she decided.

The soft twilight of New Year's Eve was blanketing the snow when a limousine pushed its aristocratic nose against the Parrish garage and blocked the sidewalk with a haughty bumper. The long space between was filled with chattering girls, a bored chauffeur and a mountain of luggage. The Parrishes flew across the snow in welcome and the front doorway mingled its white light with the colored glow of an aging Christmas tree that blinked through a window.

"It's wonderful that you could come," Penny said with a hospitable grin when they were before the fire, their bags bumping up the stairs with a cheerful Yates and their hats and coats trailing along the hall behind a helpful Bobby. "We'll dress in a minute because the boys will be here."

She looked critically at her guests. Her memory of them was vague and she was surprised at their well-bred enthusiasm. My soul, they're kind of peppy, she thought gleefully. This won't be so bad.

Nothing was ever bad to Penny; not when she was having a good time herself, for her happiness was as contagious as an epidemic. She ran from room to room, supervising an array of dresses and making all decisions on color schemes until she was satisfied. Denise, when she left her, had her mousiness hidden under red slipper-satin, and the cool perfection of Faith was lovely in green.

"She's absolutely stunning," Penny told Carrol with a swirl of admiration for her own new pink chiffon. "But you're the most beautiful of all, in white."

She pinned clusters of pale pink roses behind each ear and

turned from the mirror with an experimental shake of the head. "Remember the red rose I had stuck up on top of my hair that night at Arden? The one I didn't know how to fix and couldn't keep on? I've learned a lot since then." She surveyed herself again with the satisfied complacency of an actress ready for a sweeping entrance onto the stage, then looked higher into the mirror as Carrol stopped behind her. Brunette and blond they were reflected there; one a portrait in vivid oils, the other a drawing in soft pastels, until Penny broke the spell.

"Two lovelier femmes it would be hard to find," she said with a pleased and final nod. "Come on, let's go."

They floated down the stairs, evening sandals flashing under their trailing skirts, and Penny glanced into the dining room, full of happy pride for the flower-bedecked table and the silver candelabra above a lace cloth.

"My goodness, Trudy!" she called in a voice that cracked in agony. "Come, quick! You've got the table set all wrong. There're too many places. Didn't Mums give you the place cards?"

"Not yet, Miss Penny." Trudy hurried to the pantry door and poked her head inside. "It's that Yates, I guess. You go on in with your guests an' I'll fix it. It won't take a second."

"But the chairs are wrong and the knives and forks . . ." Penny scooped up a handful of silver and shoved it at Trudy as the doorbell rang. "Goodness, here are the boys! I'll have to go." Her dress brushed the cloth, pulled it askew as, unmindful of the havoc she had caused, she dashed into the hall.

"Hello," she greeted, interfering with Yates who was struggling under a pile of coats and caps. "I should be standing coyly in the drawing-room, but I'm not. Come on in and meet the girls."

She swung hands with Michael as she led them in and watched each face as she made her breezy introductions. The boys wore their full dress, chests and coat tails gleaming with brass buttons, and she saw that her guests were more than satisfied. "There are forty-four buttons," she told them glibly, "and you can always cut off one for a souvenir."

They grouped themselves around the fire and Dick turned to her. "How's David today?" he asked as he took the tomato juice cocktail Yates offered and hung over an enticing array of canapes. "I didn't get a chance to see him."

"He's fine." Penny selected a delectable tid-bit of shrimp and toast and nibbled it. "He thinks he'll be out in a day or two and won't have to miss much school."

"Swell." Dick, his eye on the hors d'oeuvres that were again circling toward him, watched Yates bang the plate on the coffee table and go rushing from the room as if Ali Baba and the forty thieves were after him. "What's wrong with *him?*" he asked.

"I don't know."

Everyone turned at Yates' defection. Glasses stopped in mid-air as he called over his shoulder, "He's a-comin': He's done got here!" He flung the front door wide with a flourish and a grin and announced loudly: "Here he is—Mr. Parrish, in person!"

"Hello," David said from behind his dark glasses as he stepped into the hall and set his cap, upside down, on Yates' frizzy head. "I came to the party."

"David!"

The crowd that surrounded him, that pummeled him, that hugged him and asked questions, and finally dragged him into the living room, was so riotous that Faith and Denise wondered if they would ever meet this handsome brother of Penny's. Eventually, they did. Penny remembered them— eventually.

"Now I see why we had nine places on the table," she giggled when everything was calm again and David had been piled with food and drink. "Poor old Trudy, I certainly gummed it up for her."

"It was her idea to surprise you so she shouldn't mind the extra work." David went to Carrol and shoved Dick from his place beside her. "Did you know you have two dates to-night?" he asked her.

"I have? Wonderful! But won't Jonesy mind?" Carrol spoke to David but her eyes asked the question of Bill Jones.

"No-o-o," he answered with a decided shake of his head. "Blinker's a good guy and he's only on pass until ten o'clock. I've got until twelve for mine own."

Yates swung his tray with a professional eclat, and when only the lace doily was left upon it he returned it to Trudy and announced from the door,

"Dinner is served."

CHAPTER XIV

WEST POINT HOP

"This is divine, but simply divine," Penny said to Michael who had the seat of honor at her right. "I shouldn't brag about my own party, but do you remember the one I gave at Arden when Louise acted so terribly and we were late for the hop?"

"She could stay out of my life forever," Michael answered, savoring the turkey and Trudy's famous dressing. "But to me the nicest part of this meal is that I can eat it without wonder-ing when a thick water glass is going to hit me, and can lean back when I want to." He stretched his legs under the table and encountered Dick who had the same idea.

"Mr. Dumbjohn!" Steve shouted from the other end of the table, so suddenly that Dick jerked upright with a feeble, "Yes, sir."

They laughed, and Dick made a face and slid down again. "Not here, my friend," he bragged. "You're a big guy in barracks, but you can't bother me here. In fact, I'm more at ease than you are because I know the family better."

"You'll regret that crack tomorrow." Steve wagged a finger at him. "You're going to be oh, so sorry you got fresh."

"It's worth it." Dick attacked his dinner and explained his troubles to Faith between bites.

When it was time for the dance, Penny slipped into her new fur coat and admired its soft ripples beside the white fox of Denise and the ermine that wrapped Faith. "We look just as cute," she whispered to Carrol who wore her squirrel, carelessly and without envy of the evening furs about her. "But they look like something out of Vogue or Harper's Bazaar. I'll bet their coats belong to their mothers."

"Probably." Carrol hid a smile as she watched Penny make transportation arrangements.

"You can drive our big car, Carrol, and I'll take mine," Penny said importantly. "So divide up any way you want to."

David went to tell Trudy good-by and to see the children, and the others paired off in the garage. Penny backed her car along the crackling ice of the driveway and gave a hurrying toot for David.

"Aren't you glad we're us?" she asked her passengers as they cruised off into the night.

The dance in her extravagant language, was "divine, but simply divine." The gymnasium was ablaze with lights, gay with girls in bright new Christmas dresses and formal with white gloved cadets in their gray with shining brass buttons.

"I wish the dance could have been in Cullem Hall," Penny

chatted while the boys were checking the wraps, "but of course it couldn't be because the plebes aren't allowed in it." She sighed, then welcomed Michael who was charting a weaving course through couples eager for dancing or bound for the movie theatre that opened its doors into the wide hall. He gave her a small folder of dance programme, held together by a silk cord of entwined gray and gold and black, and she read it with a pleased glance before she stampeded her guests through the door to the ballroom.

Carrol took her card from Jonesy and suppressed her curiosity about its contents until she had been presented by a very formal and respectful cadet to the chaperones. If I thought the hop at Fort Arden was queer, she thought, this is even rarer. There it was a gay mixture of all ages, a free catch as catch can, and here it is so formal that it's almost frightening.

She turned to watch Denise and Faith who were staring blankly at their bits of pasteboard. Faith glanced from hers to the dancing couples, to the orchestra and the balcony that encircled the room; but Denise, wide-eyed and speechless, was staring at Steve's snowy finger as it moved across the neat script that forecast her twelve dances for the evening. He thrust the card into her hand, said politely, "Shall we dance?" and her eyes jerked up to sweep across the scene before her. A smile lit up her small face until it glowed.

"Oh, let's!" she cried, holding out her arms like a child reaching for a lollypop. "I've never been so happy in my life."

"Well, you never can tell," Jonesy said to Carrol with a shake of his head. "I thought she was a complete blank until she suddenly caught the spirit of the thing. She has a baby doll technique that only needs a southern accent."

"She really is sincere," Carrol answered as she slid into his arms and controlled the glance she longed to send back to David. "I suppose this is the most fun the girl has ever had. Her family keeps her wrapped in perfume-scented wool."

"Goose down, I'll bet," he said in her ear as he swung her across the floor. "She looks that way."

He danced well and the soft strains of the opening waltz held hidden glamour. They wove in and out among the dancers and when the music stopped, Carrol was surprised to find herself by the door again. "Blinker gets the next half," Jonesy said magnanimously. "You weren't hoping for it, were you?"

"I wasn't even wondering," Carrol's answer was truthful and she added, "I was just enjoying it, completely."

"Thanks. That was a swell answer and it makes me wish I hadn't parted with so many dances. Let's see." He reached up for her programme which in copy of five hundred others, dangled by its cord from a knobby brass button on his left shoulder. "I've got the second, and the fourth is a no-break, and I gave that to Blinker. The seventh is, too; and darn it, he gets that if he's still here. After that I have clear sailing."

He motioned to David and grinned at the ease with which a pair of dark glasses singled them out, and drifted away. "I'll meet you over in that corner where you said your company sets up headquarters," he called as they passed him. David nodded, and they whirled on.

The evening ticked away; rhythmically with the music's beat, rapidly with the throbbing of hearts, and slowly with the dreaminess of waltz time.

"This is a moonlight," David said when he came to claim his fourth dance, "so I think I can safely park my glasses. Are you having fun?"

"I'm loving every minute of it," Carrol answered as lights dimmed and colored spotlights began their play across the slowly moving couples. "Isn't it beautiful?"

"Would you like to go up on the balcony and look down on it?"

"Let's do!"

They circled slowly to the door and ran up the stairs.

"There's Penny, right below us," Carrol pointed as they sat down and looked over the rail. David turned his chair until he was facing her instead of the throng below and, when her eyes had swept over the long room, she asked thoughtfully, "Were you frightened, David?"

"Sometimes I was. Not frightened exactly, but worried about the future and afraid that I'd never see you again, and wishing that I'd looked at you oftener when I had the chance."

She knew that he was looking at her now and, although her eyes were still following Penny, her heart was tapping against the white chiffon of her frock as she asked, "Did you get straightened out about our foolish Thanksgiving misunderstanding?"

"Partly." David kept her waiting for her answer. "I knew I'd been an awful sap to think I could shut myself away from life like a hermit or a monk; but the funny part of it was that I forgot about you—about the fact that I was going to leave you free, I mean—and only felt mad at myself for being such an ass. Of course, I knew it was a good thing that I'd made the break," he hurried to add, "since I might be all washed up for a career."

"But you didn't make a break." Carrol's eyes forsook the view below for a teasing look at David. "You were just being high and mighty—and nothing happened."

"You mean . . ." David leaned forward, all bristling indignation. "Do you mean to say that you paid no attention to my dropping you out of my affairs?"

"Not a bit." She shook her head and shrugged. "Not any more than Tippy would if Bobby told her she couldn't ever play with him again."

"Well, I'll be darned." David sat back and laughed. "Why didn't you say so?"

"I told Penny. And I saved the amusing letter you wrote me. It certainly was stuffy! And I made some very fine resolutions myself."

"What were they?"

"They don't matter now because your being sick changed everything." Carrol rested an elbow on the rail and laid her cheek in her cupped palm. "Do you remember the ride we took last summer?" she asked, turning her eyes to him in long, slow inquiry. "When we started out by disliking each other and ended up by saying that we'd be pals, as Penny and I are? With no foolishness? Well, we've made a lot of foolishness," she ended severely.

"But we've gone past just being pals; I have at least."

"Perhaps. But that needn't bother us now. The point is, that we had a grand understanding of each other that day, and that's what we have to keep. Always. It's no good if we get mad and jealous and hurt over every little thing."

"I think you've got something there." David clasped his hands between his knees and leaned forward. "We ought to be more like Mums and Dad, sort of jogging along . . ."

"Oh, David, you're too ridiculous." Carrol leaned away from him and frowned. "First you're going to have nothing more to do with me, and now you've got me as old as your mother. My goodness! You *are* mixed up in your mind."

"Well, who wouldn't be with you around!" David gave her chair a jiggle and leaned his arms on the rail beside her. "You get me so darned confused . . ."

"Then it's a good thing the doctor is making you go out for athletics in a big way. By the time you finish baseball and swimming and a few sets of tennis, you won't have time to mull over life and its problems. Look, there's Penny again."

The music stopped and Penny, below them, glanced up to wave. "Stay where you are," she called. "Jonesy and I are coming up."

Her slippers tapped on the stairs and with a skipping hop for Jonesy's long stride she danced along the balcony. "I've never had such a good time!" she cried, swirling her pink skirts over a chair and leaning her head back. "Michael says that Faith and Denise are getting perfectly marvelous cuts for new girls. About a dozen cadets have asked to be introduced to them."

"And you seem to be doing all right." Jonesy turned to David to complain. "I can't get five steps with the girl. Two feet of rumba and a bar of fox-trot . . ." he broke off to frown at Carrol . . . "and what do you mean by hiding up here in the balcony," he scolded. "I wish you'd remember that you're my drag."

"It's my poor health," David explained. "I'm not strong like other boys and she had to see that I rested."

"Phooey!" Jonesy searched unsuccessfully in both cuffs for his handkerchief and mopped his forehead with a glove. "You've done nothing but rest while I waited on you." The music began again and he caught Carrol's hand and pulled her to her feet. "You can sit up here and rest this one," he told David, "and we won't even be thinking of you."

"Aw, Jonesy, have a heart," David protested. "It's half-past nine now and I won't get that seventh dance with Carrol."

"You should have thought of that before you went blind," Jonesy flung back, pulling Carrol along with him. "Maybe Steve or some of your classmates will loosen up with an encore."

"I'll cut in on you," David threatened, hanging over the stairway.

"Oh, no you won't." Jonesy's deep bass cracked into chuckles. "You won't be able to catch us."

"Have you danced with Denise or Faith?" Penny asked in true sisterly fashion as David came back to her.

"Can't. My health, you know." David planted himself in his chair again and Penny stood behind him, glaring down on the back of his head.

"Well, you might cut in for at least a few steps."

"Can't," he repeated. "Doctor's orders." He slumped in his chair, peering under the rail for a couple who would be the captain of the football team and a girl in a white dress, and was deaf to Penny's pleas.

"But, David," she coaxed, resorting to flattery. "They're my guests and they think you're so handsome."

"They couldn't. Not in those awful specs."

"Well, they did. And those aren't 'awful specs.' They're good, ground glass, and they cost me three dollars."

"You got stung." David's eyes had found Carrol and were following her contentedly. "Run along; you bother me."

Penny's lips tightened. "If you'd look at my dance card that's down there hung on Michael," she snapped, "you'd see that I'm only here because I'm hooked up with you for this dance—at least until the encore."

"My dear child, I'm so sorry." David sprang up and placed a chair for her. "Have a seat."

"At the first plebe hop I ever got to? I will not." Penny anchored a foot that twitched to stamp. "I've waited on you hand and foot, David Parrish, and now you can march yourself right down stairs with me."

"All right, dear," David answered meekly as he took one last look below. The piece was nearing an end, the couple he watched was spotted, so he took Penny's hand and hustled her to the stairs.

"We have fun, don't we Blinker, dear?" she cooed, cuddling her fingers in his. "I like having you cross and funny as you used to be."

"Um." David put his arm around her, peered above her head, and shoved her along at a break-neck pace.

She tried to match his stride for a few bars then pulled him to a stop and said breathlessly: "This is a dance—not a marathon."

"Got to get to the other end of the hall." David forced her on and, in spite of her irritation, Penny giggled. She saw Faith dancing ahead of her and, by skillful maneuvering, ended the dance beside her and beside a stag line that held cadets she knew. A smile flung across David's shoulder brought one out, and a quick twist of her arm that was linked in David's, threw him face to face with a smiling and unsuspecting Faith.

"The dance was lots of fun, brother dear," she said when she saw his white glove in the correct center of Faith's green waist. "Remember not to overtire yourself."

The look David shot her was murderous, and the first words she said to a blinking and dazed partner were, "Isn't it lovely that he forgot to put on his glasses?"

"I beg your pardon?"

"His dark glasses. David just got over being blind, you know." Penny laughed at the stricken look that met her words and found herself embellishing upon the horror of David's illness while she went around and around the gym at a gallop. The admirers of Faith whom she had boasted about seemed to have melted into ghosts for, when the whirling dervish who had her in a wrestler's grip side-swiped David, the smiling misery on David's face so upset her that she disastrously missed a beat.

"It was lots of fun," she panted joyfully when a solid bulk of gray stopped their gyrations and a heaven-sent voice said, "May I break?" Michael loomed large and restful and she fell gratefully into his arms.

"Run, quick, and relieve David," she gasped when she could catch her breath. "Just leave me anywhere. He only has about five minutes left and he's having a fit. Hurry."

She watched Michael weave his way across the floor before she leaned against a wall and looked down to see if her feet were intact. "The crazy idiot," she groaned as she slipped a sandal off, only to slip it on again as a cadet from David's company stopped before her. "I didn't mean you," she explained, guilty at having been caught talking to herself. "It was . . . but never mind, I've recovered now."

She saw Carrol walking along the hall with David and relaxed in the enjoyment of her own affairs.

"Do you think you can make it in time?" Carrol was asking as David swung himself into his overcoat. "You have only three minutes."

"I'll make it." He fastened the collar under his chin, snatched the cap she carried and bolted the few feet to the door. As she watched him he whirled around, ran back and ended with a slide before her. "G'by," he said, grinning; then he was gone.

The rest of the dance Carrol found, was flat. Denise and Faith and Penny seemed to find it entertaining enough for, when the lights dimmed and Army Blue foretold the end of the evening, they sighed and danced with lingering slowness.

White gloves spattered applause and, as the hands on all watches clung together for that brief second that marks the passing of a year, a cheer leader mounted the orchestra's dais and the voices of the cadets resounded against the walls in the *Long Corps*. A new year had been welcomed in.

"I wish we could do it all over again," Denise said as she walked beside Steve to the parking place.

"You can, any week-end you'll come up," he answered.

"Really? Why, Steve!" Denise stopped in the snow. Against the white her red dress looked like a Christmas candle and her small face was a flame above soft fur.

"Of course it will be a first class hop," he said proudly. "But I think you'll like it even better."

"I'll adore it, and thank you. I hope I can come soon," she rattled on, and got reluctantly into the car beside Penny.

"We'll all be over tomorrow afternoon," Dick said in a last salute to Faith. "You won't go home until evening, will you?"

"They'll be here." Penny slipped off her brake and leaned toward the gray fingers that hovered between the two cars. "It seems awfully mean to drive off and leave you to walk home in the cold," she said.

"Don't give it a thought," Jonesy shivered with a rattling of his teeth that sounded like castanets. "Next year as a young lieutenant, I'm going to spend my time riding around in cars after ten o'clock."

Other cadets were trudging down the hill in the snow, taxis were pulling out, and only a few couples were braving the ice for the extra minutes that would take them to the bottom of the hill.

"Penny, you don't know how lucky you are, living up here," Denise said later as she sat on the rug before a cheerfully burning fire and kicked off her sandals.

"Oh, yes I do." Penny in her stocking feet, was setting a plate of turkey sandwiches in the center of the group. She crawled back to a tray that held a pitcher and glasses and began pouring out cold milk. "Any time any of you want to park, come on up."

"I've got a future date," Denise proclaimed proudly. "Believe it or not—I can't."

"With Steve?" Faith curled her feet under her and leaned her back against the divan. At Denise's triumphant nod she laughed and said: "Well, you did better than I did. You got a first classman, and I only got Dick."

"He'll last three years longer and you've both gone over with a bang. My goodness." Penny was pleased through a large bite of sandwich. "Lot's of girls come up on blind dates and are never asked back. Aren't you proud of them, Carrol?"

"I'm thrilled to death." Carrol looked at Denise and asked slyly: "Would you rather do this or read plays?"

"Oh, my gosh." Faith's surprising slang, erupting from her cameo-cut mouth, sent them into gales of laughter, and it was two o'clock before they stumbled sleepily up the stairs.

"It's wonderful to have a crowd again," Penny yawned, cuddling under her pink down comfort and watching Carrol opening the window she had forgotten. "I've missed that here at West Point. We had such fun at Arden, and now I zip back and forth to school so fast I never get to know any girls."

"I'm glad we have them, too." Carrol swung back the cranes that held the drapes and switched off the dressing table lights. "How does it happen," she asked as she fumbled on tired feet through the dark, "that you always manage to get in bed first and leave me all the dirty work?"

CHAPTER XV

PRELUDE TO JUNE WEEK

Following the Christmas holidays, the long dull weeks that are known by cadets as "the gloom period," dragged their weary way into spring. First classmen's tempers were short, second classmen's nerves were strained, and third classmen, remembering this time from the year before, felt it their sacred duty to make the plebes suffer outwardly for the others' inward impatience. The Hudson was gray with floating cakes of ice, small thwarted icebergs that sought a larger life in the ocean; the Post was gray from coal smoke; and Mrs. Parrish thought she was turning gray from running what she and Trudy called "the Parrish hotel."

Girls came for one week-end and lingered on until the next one; relatives came to see the sights and to get away from their own cold and ugly towns; and David's friends spent all their spare minutes snatching naps on her divans, her chairs, or sprawled on her rugs. "It's got to get better," she told herself as Yates took leaves from the dining room table, only to put them back with others added. "It can't get worse."

But it did. It got much worse because, quite suddenly, it turned hot. Buds appeared on the trees and burst frantically into leaf, trying to make small umbrellas for the grass that was being scorched by an over-zealous sun. Summer clothes were dragged from chests and, between the feeding and entertaining of guests, the feminine Parrishes rushed into New York in search of summer silks and cotton tub frocks.

"If it weren't for David I'd stop right here and have a nervous break-up," Marjorie Parrish said to her husband one sizzling afternoon as she climbed up on the bleachers to watch a plebe baseball game. "I'm so grateful the glasses Penny gave him are on my nose instead of his that I can bear anything."

"After we get June Week over you can rest all summer," Major Parrish told her, adding a lusty cheer for David who had laid a neat bunt halfway between the pitcher and the catcher.

"If I live through June Week." She stood up to see David trot back to the bench, out, but satisfied to have sent a runner on to second, and smiled down on him proudly. "Goodness, he's brown," she said as she sat down on the narrow boards again. "Do you suppose he stands very high in his class?"

"We won't know definitely until after his finals." Major Parrish was watching Penny who was waving from below them.

"The guests have all gone," Penny shouted. "Isn't it lovely? All but Carrol, and she just came. I'm going back for her as soon as she changes her dress."

"Fine." Mrs. Parrish smiled and nodded and returned to her subject of David. "We watch him play baseball, we watch him win swimming meets and be top man on the tennis squad, and I wish I could give Colonel Pearson a silk purse filled with golden coins like the knights of old did."

Major Parrish nodded, his eyes on the game, and she looked across the baseball diamond at row after row of tents that had been erected under watchful trees. "In just a few days David will be in one of those," she said happily, her mind wandering to June Week now that David wasn't on the field. "He'll be a third classman, by Jimminy. Are you listening to me?"

"Umhum. He'll be a third classman and heckling some other mother's boy. Are you going to let him?"

"Let him! I don't suppose I'll ever have the chance to *let* David do anything again. From now on I'll have to concentrate on Bobby. That was a nice catch the boy in right field made, wasn't it?"

"Very nice. That was your son."

"Oh, Mercy! I'll have to be more enthusiastic."

She settled down contentedly; and if, as the difficult days boiled along, her enthusiasm could have helped cadets win their letters in sports or pass their final examinations, West Point would have been overrun with athletes and the classes would have had a very small middle and no bottom.

Penny cheered for them, too, when she had time, for her own examinations were in the offing and she muttered dates at the breakfast table and growled at David because his work was going smoothly.

"Listen, play-girl," he teased one afternoon when he had taken off his blouse and was prepared for comfort in the cool living room, "if you had kept up with your work like I did you wouldn't be in such a state."

"And get sick? No thank you. I don't care where I stand, anyway, so long as I know enough to help me in my career." Penny slammed her book shut and skidded it across the table. "I've got so much else on my mind right now."

"What?" David flattened himself on the divan and hung

his legs over the arm. His white shirt was open at the throat, but even relaxed and recumbent he was careful of the crease in his trousers. "What under the sun could you have on your mind if you had a mind to have it on?"

"Well, that's a flattering speech." Penny made a face at him then laughed. "It's beds, if you must know."

"Beds? What beds?"

"The beds that Faith and Denise are going to sleep in June Week, plus the beds the Prescotts are going to need if they come, to say nothing of a few saved out for the family and Carrol and me."

"Are the Prescott's coming?" David lifted his head. "Who said they were coming?"

"You know they're coming because you heard Mummy read the letter. Or maybe you weren't here." Penny's love for being the Paul Revere of the family spurred her into a gallop, and she imparted the news before David might remember that he had heard it somewhere.

"Mrs. Prescott wrote that Bob got into the Point all right and that he's already come east for a couple of months of special coaching, and that they're taking a trip and would like to see June Week." She said it all in one breath and David burst out,

"With all those kids? My gosh, Mums can't take care of that mob!"

"Oh, an aunt or someone is going to keep Jack and Jerry at Arden and only Mary is coming with them. Perhaps Major and Mrs. Prescott will stay at the hotel or somewhere and just Mary will be here."

"I'll be glad to see old Bob again," David said, putting his arms under his head and stretching luxuriously, "I don't envy him the next year, though."

"How long have you to go before you're a yearling, Mr. Dumbguard?" Penny asked with a grin.

"Two hundred and sixty-four hours and fifty-nine seconds, sir," David answered automatically. "Poor old Bob."

"Will you haze him, David?"

"Might. I don't know. Bob's a good kid, and he's the kind it might go hard with. He's sensitive and shy. I suppose I'll just recognize him and let it go."

He closed his eyes and Penny wriggled with delight to hear him talking with a voice of authority. "My brother, who is a yearling," she practised, "wants us to go up to Delafield to swim or into the Boodlers' for a coke." She grinned to herself and forgot her beds, and only came back into the present when she heard her beloved car call to her with its very special purr as it came up the hill.

How well she finished her school year depended on her teachers' liking for her and their imagination. Her examination papers, that were brief in spots, might wander on for pages when a subject caught her fancy, and more ink stained her fingers than darkened the paper. She struggled her way through, however, and dumped her books in her car with amused smiles following her, and the hopes from a departure-speeding group of spinster-teachers that she would be with them again next year.

Happily she trundled homeward, the little car ticking comfortably at its allotted forty miles an hour and the countryside covered with her song.

"I'm free!" she shouted as she flung her books inside the door. "Why don't you run to greet your daughter just home from the penitentiary?" Silence answered her and she ran up the stairs and along the hall. Strange luggage cluttered up her room, and in her open closet dresses she recognized as Faith's and Denise's were squeezed against Carrol's, and others she had never seen before draped the door.

Ah, she thought, a stranger in our midst. Without shame she rummaged through an open toilet case and ploughed among the contents of an overcrowded drawer. "Mary

Prescott!" she exclaimed when a familiar pair of shorts was uncovered. "I wonder where they've gone."

She peeped into the sleeping porch, stole time enough to find and ink large squares of cardboard and, with the aid of bobby pins and bits of string, placarded the five-cot dormitory.

"Mary, Carrol, Faith, Denise, and me," she read from the foot of each bed. "We look like a girls' camp." That gave her another brilliant idea, so, filching one more cardboard from the bosom of her father's freshly laundered shirts, she contrived a sign that was a masterpiece.

"CAMP BEAUTY REST" she tacked into the white woodwork above the door; and in small parentheses beneath it, "(No beast must enter.)"

She combed her hair and began to wonder where she could trace her wandering household. In her car once more, she cut tracks in hot asphalt that ended at the tennis courts.

A match was on, and from the little crowd that sat on grandstands watching, Penny knew it was plebe finals. She parked her car beside the drill field and ran across the street. Mary met her with a rush and from the entanglement of arms, Penny hit a round, smooth cheek with a resounding kiss.

"Just the same old Mary," she exclaimed as they both rubbed their noses and blinked back the tears that smarted. "I didn't mean to knock you down."

"I've been bowled over ever since I got here," Mary laughed, "so it doesn't matter. Boy, it's wonderful!" Her clear gray eyes were just as sweet as ever and the sandy hair that was drawn down into a roll was neat compared with Penny's flying locks.

"Are your mother and father here?"

"Why, don't you know?" Mary linked her arm in Penny's. "They're staying over at Gladstone; and your mother and the children are, too; and your father is going over every night."

"Well, my soul, why doesn't somebody tell me these things?" Penny laughed, and Mary went on to explain.

"It happened so suddenly that your mother left a note on the living room table."

"I didn't go in there." They were walking across the grass and Penny skipped happily. "Isn't it wonderful? We can have a house party with plenty of room, and Mums can get a rest from us. The poor dear's awfully tired."

"That's what Mr. Houghton thought, and Carrol took them all back in the station wagon so your big car would be on this end for your father, and we could have the other one. Isn't it thrilling," she exclaimed admiringly, "to have a car of your own?"

"Isn't it?" Penny stopped to hug her again and to wave to Denise and Faith. "And isn't it thrilling to have you here! Did you meet the girls?"

"We all came over together and I liked them. They knew how to call out Dick and Michael so they'll be over pretty soon too. I've never been so excited in my life." She looked at Penny. "Is Louise here?"

"No." Penny's tone was short. "But you can bet she will be. She's been a pain to me all winter."

"So I gathered from your letters. She won't be staying with us, will she?"

"Oh, goodness, I hope not!" Penny sighed and for the second time rejoiced that her mother would be elsewhere. "If Mums were here she'd be sure to get weak and let her in. I have so much to talk about. . . ." She saw Dick and Michael joining Faith and Denise, so prodded Mary on. After another jubilant reunion they climbed up on the bleachers, and Penny asked Michael, "How's it going?"

"Faith told me that David's doing all right. He got the first two sets and lost the third. Boy, what a back-hand that guy's got. I'd hate to have him fire one of those shots at me." He leaned forward to watch and Penny smiled contentedly down the row.

"Game. Set." The referee from his tower beside the court leaned down and David and his opponent met each other at the net.

"That makes it two and two," Dick said, watching them mop their faces at a water bucket. "I hope they finish up before we have supper call."

David served, lobbed, smashed his way along; and while Penny watched him now and then, she had so much to say to Mary, that he had to fight his way to victory without her usual help.

"Set. Match," the referee called. And Dick and Michael went clattering down the boards.

David released his opponent's shoulders and came toward them with a wide grin for Mary. He took their congratulations calmly and laughed away their compliments. "It really doesn't matter," he said. "Cochrane's a swell player and we'll be teamed together in the doubles. How are you, Mary?"

"I'm fine. And Bob said to tell you hello. You don't look as if you'd been sick."

"I don't feel it." David wiped his forehead on the short sleeve of his shirt and looked around the group. "Where's Carrol?"

"Gone to take the family to Gladstone. Isn't it grand, David, that we're to have the house to ourselves?" Penny pushed close to him and inserted herself into the conversation. "Did you know about it?"

"Yes, Dad told me before he left. I've got to run now, but I'll see you tomorrow." He took his racket from Dick who was showing Faith how he could twist himself into a pretzel and still beat David.

"It's form that does it," Dick was saying when the racket was lifted from his upraised hand and he was left standing like a winged Mercury without his torch. "Hey, are you fellows going back to camp?"

"I didn't know you'd moved to Camp Clinton, David!" Penny cried. "When did you do it?"

"Yesterday. It's a lot cooler than barracks, and any old grad can bunk in my room and welcome. Come on, Dick, and stop showing off."

"I'm coming, Blinker. But you don't need to be so cocky. Just because he won a fiddlin' little game of tennis," he said in what he considered a very prissy tone, "he thinks he can order me around." He departed, backwards, until Michael swung him around; then the three trotted their stiff little trot toward their new camp.

The girls got into Penny's car. At home the house was cool and peaceful, and only Trudy's humming broke the quiet.

"We might still sleep on the porch," Penny suggested when they were upstairs and crowded into her room. "We'll want to talk at night and it's cooler, but we can spread out our dresses."

She rushed about shoving the absent members' clothes along the closet rods and emptying drawers. "Denise," she called, "you and Faith can take the guest room; and Mary, Tippy's room is ready. I think we'd better skip Bobby's den of horrors because it's always such a mess, and toads and things might come crawling out at night. And anyway, Carrol and I are used to falling over each other." She blocked the attic stairs with Tippy's treasures, closed the door to her mother and father's room, and returned to her own in time to find them laughing at her sign.

"Camp Beauty Rest is marvelous," Mary said, calling to the others to try the beds that bore their names. "Although I don't suppose we'll do much resting and we won't dare admit the 'beauty' fits us. Still, it's cute."

They scattered shoes and odds and ends along the hall, and

Penny, hindering more than helping, pitched them in wherever they would fit.

"There's a box down here for you, Miss Penny," Trudy called when they were lying on their beds resting from their labors. "I done forgot about it till jes' now."

"What kind of box?" Penny bounced off the bed and tore down the stairs.

A cardboard carton sat on the kitchen table surrounded by the dinner Trudy was preparing, and Penny snatched it up. "My goodness, it's full of little packages," she said with a thrill. "Who brought it?"

"Mr. Jones; that cadet who came to dinner. He jes' left it and went away. He said you'd understand."

"Well, I don't, but thanks." Penny bore the box along the hall and, seeing Carrol parking in the drive, ran to the door. "How do you do?" she called. "Did you get the family settled?"

"They're in." Carrol snatched her purse from the seat and ran across the lawn. "Your mother said she'd plan the meals and keep an eye on us." She skipped up the steps and saw the carton. "What's that?"

"I don't know. Trudy said Jonesy brought it and I was about to go upstairs and unpack it. Come on, let's hurry."

They took the box into Camp Beauty Rest and Penny dumped it on Mary's bed. "Gather around," she invited. "I have a present."

She opened the cover and lifted out one of the small packages. A card was tucked under the paper ribbon that tied it and "Denise" was written on it. "One, two, three, four, five," Penny counted quickly. "We must each have something. Oh, boy!" She gave Denise the package and fished about for the others. When she came to her own, the card bore Michael's scrawl and he had written: "We don't know who Mary's drag will be, so Dave and Dick and I have fixed her up."

"Someone open quickly," Penny begged as she pitched a box to Carrol. "I'm about to die from curiosity."

"Here goes mine." Faith slipped off the wrapping. "June Week favors," she cried, holding up a gold compact. "And underneath is a June Week programme."

The others tore away their papers, and Mary's bed sagged on its springs as they crowded onto it. "I got a compact, too," Penny squealed. "Just like the one David gave Carrol for Christmas. Has yours got the West Point crest on it?"

"Umhum." Mary held up hers. "Aren't the boys lambs to think of me? What did you get, Carrol?"

"An evening bag; a gold one with the crest. And Denise has one, too. Who sent you yours, Denise?"

"Steve." Denise's mouse teeth, that didn't seem so mousy any more, flashed in a wide smile. "Faith, is yours from Dick?"

"It is; the crazy nut." Faith was reading her card and laughing. "He says, 'Roses are red, violets are blue, and here is something the government bought for you.' What is that supposed to mean, Penny?"

"Nothing. He probably had to draw the money out of his cadet fund. That's the deposit the government makes for the cadets every month, just as if they were soldiers; and he likes to sound impressive. Let's read the programmes."

They picked up the small white leather booklets that gave the date and the hour of June Week events, and Penny looked at Denise. "I should think you'd feel ashamed," she grumbled. "You can go to every single thing because you're with a first classman, while the rest of us are going to have a stuffy time."

"Oh, no we're not." Carrol waved a note from David. "He says Bill Henderson has nobly offered himself, and Jonesy will look after us until his drag gets here for the last two days; and he has a couple of other men in mind. That sounds all right for those who want to flit."

"Of whom I suppose you will not be one," Penny laughed

at her. "You probably want to sit under a tree and watch Blinker zipping around Camp Clinton and dashing hither, thither and thence."

"Oh, I'll be flitting with the rest of you." Carrol looked at her note again and smiled at David's noble plea that read, 'I really wish you would go places.' "I'll probably be ready first and waiting on the doorstep."

Laughter greeted her remark and Penny flopped across the bed at the sound of Trudy's voice.

"Miss Penny." Trudy, in the door, was plaintive. "I've been a-callin' an' a-callin' you to dinner, an' the telephome's been ringin', an' someone is awaitin' to speak to Miss Denise."

Trudy's voice sounded dismal but they knew she was enjoying all the fun, so Denise pulled her to the cluttered bed before she dashed through Mrs. Parrish's room to the phone that stood on a bedside table.

"Hey, Mary," she called. "Want a date for the movies tonight?"

"Do I! Just ask me. Who is it with, with whom?" Mary answered.

"Jonesy. Shall I tell him yes?"

"Tell him yes." Mary sang out the words then looked at Penny. "Is it all right if I go?" she asked.

"Of course, darling." Penny waved Carrol's evening bag before Trudy, then clutched her around the waist and nuzzled her head into Trudy's white apron. "They're mean to me," she sobbed with heaving shoulders. "They go off with first classmen and I should think you'd make them take me with them."

"I'll take you down to dinner and make you eat oatmeal like Tippy does if you don't stop rumplin' me." Trudy pushed Penny back and smoothed her apron. "Don't you think you could come down an' eat," she coaxed, "so's Yates can take himself to somethin' in town he wants to do?"

"We'll come, my sweet." Penny gave Trudy another hug

and asked with an uptilted smile, "Do I look as if I have the measles now?"

"You look like you got a bird's nest in your hair." She hurried out and the girls flanked her in a noisy escort down the stairs.

Later, Mary and Denise drove off to the gymnasium and their movie dates and, lying under the stars, Penny said, "This makes me think of a sorority house. I've never been in one, but I've heard that girls are always coming and going and there's lots of excitement. Oh-oh, there goes the telephone."

She scrambled up to tell her mother that they were alive and well, and when she threw herself on the grass again, announced as David might have done:

"Sir, it is exactly eleven hours and forty-six minutes until June Week."

CHAPTER XVI

JUNE WEEK

The third day of June dawned exactly on the dot, and the sun that heralded it into being was round and red and jovial. Dew sparkle on the grass, trees waved their fans lazily over Camp Clinton and, from the area of barracks, a bugle sounded. June Week had begun.

"What's the cannon booming for?" Carrol asked later in the morning, looking along the cots in the sleeping porch.

"It's a salute to some important visitor, I guess." Penny sat up in bed and blinked. "How many times did it fire?"

"Forever, it seemed to me."

"Then it's probably a Secretary of War or State or something, or a visiting general."

The gun continued its salute at intervals for the entire week; and cars drew up before the Thayer Hotel that stood just inside the gates, unloading mothers and fathers of the graduating class or army officers back for their reunions. Its lobby was filled with girls, bright in dirndls and prints, always dashing in or out, rushing to meet cadets who wore the special June Week uniform of white trousers and gray full-dress coat, with smart white cap above it. They danced away the tea hours, caught hurried swims at Delafield; and there was never a vacant table in the Boodlers'.

Reviews, parades, and ceremonies. Music floating across starry nights from three great ballrooms. Proud parents watching sons receive awards.

Camp Clinton marched to bugles, kept its equipment neat with its accustomed practice; but Camp Beauty Rest defied all laws of order. In spite of Penny's careful allotting of beds and dressingrooms, shoes were always lost and dresses rarely reached their closets. Every morning Trudy looked at the array and tried to guess their owners by the sizes. No one seemed to care. When Faith's green linen came across the parade ground on Mary, Carrol's blue sharkskin was sitting in the Boodlers' with Penny's yellow print, while Carrol and Penny cut through the waves in two strange bathing suits.

"Really," Mary said from under the bed on the afternoon of Graduation Parade, "I did have two red shoes. I know I did because I was with Mother when she bought them for me, and I saw Penny wearing them last night."

"Not me, pet." Penny crawled under to help her look.

"I'd have about as much chance of wearing your shoes as I would Tippy's." She found the shoes in the wastebasket, their soles still smooth from never having been worn, and presented them to Mary, wrapped in tissue paper. "There," she said with satisfaction. "I hope that proves my innocence."

"It does, my child, and thank you." Mary took the shoes as Carrol called from downstairs.

"We're going to be late for the parade. Isn't *anyone* ready to go yet?"

"I am." Penny smoothed her curls and ran down the stairs. "We'll save you places if we can," she shouted as she dashed out of the door. "You can bring my car."

When she and Carrol squeezed into the crowd that faced the barracks, first call was blowing. "Here they come," Penny cried. "I think this parade is the most thrilling thing of all June Week!"

From Camp Clinton, diagonally across the plain, marched the second class and the plebes. The sunlight glinted on their breast plates and their bayonets; and there was the swish, swish, swish, of starched trousers as every white-clad leg, every gray-coated arm swung in perfect rhythm. On and on they came to join their corpsmates. When they reached the roadway by the barracks, hearts in the fourth class were beating high. The third class joined the ranks as usual, but the first class formed along the outside of the lines as file closers. Maroon sashes, shakos with their eagle-feathered plumes erect and fluttering in the breeze, gave color to the ranks as cadet captains and lieutenants took their places.

"Rest!" The command rang out.

The coveted moment for the plebes had come. Rifles were lowered from their shoulders, and their hands reached out to clasp the hand of fellowship first classmen offered. Up and down the line the first class hurried. Time was short. Some faces beamed in a rapturous glow, other eyes were suspiciously wet; and David, when the first captain met him with a smiling grip, knew that all his suffering had been worth it. Jonesy and Steve were formal in their seconds of recognition, but Jonesy winked and Steve added extra pressure in his handshake.

Again the bugles blew from across the plain.

Chin straps were pulled down as quick commands barked out. The distant band began to play the beloved Army Blue; and company by company, battalion by battalion, the line broke into a column and marched onto the Plain.

"Hurry!" Penny cried, catching Carrol's hand in hers.

They ran around the parade ground and joined the throng of spectators who for several hours had occupied an improvised grandstand or waited on the grass. The corps was stretched its length across the field. The band was playing its formal way along the line and back again, while West Point stood rigidly at attention. It was the second parade of the day and the long rays of the sun were burning down. Here and there a tired cadet dropped to the ground, was whisked away by comrades, and the band returned to its position.

"Present arms!"

The hush that followed the command was broken only by the thud of hands against the rifle stocks. The sunset gun boomed in the silence. With stirring tones, the National Anthem filled the air; and high above the tree tops, the Stars and Stripes billowed out against the sky before they slid slowly down into the green. A faint sigh shook the watching throng, and many eyes were misty as the great folds were caught in waiting arms.

"Penny," Carrol whispered, her arms stiff against her sides, "do you remember the flag at Arden, and David saying that no matter *where* we went, we'd find it?"

Penny nodded mutely and thought of all the years the flag had waved above her happy carelessness. Her heart was full, and a moment that she longed to keep was gone. First classmen were already stepping from the ranks and forming behind their cadet officers; a long thin ribbon of them stretched before the corps. Their salute was rendered to the Commandant; his answering salute returned; and when their caps and shakos were once more adjusted, they faced about for the greatest tribute their four years had earned.

"Pass in review!" the command was given.

The band blared forth again. Under the new command of the ranking second classman the corps passed before schoolmates who would never march with it again. Guidons dipped in bright salute and "eyes right" turned the heads in every swinging company as the gray and white swept along the plain. Past the watching crowd they went, across the street, and through the sally-port into the area. Graduation Parade was over.

"Golly," Penny said humbly when the last man disappeared. "It makes me feel so envious of David, and so little and so useless."

"I know what you mean," Carrol nodded. "If we were boys we'd want to come to West Point and then be in the Army. It's big and wonderful and it fills us with a kind of awe; but we're important, too."

"Yes, I guess we are." Penny looked out across the empty parade ground. "It's just that I've always taken the flag and everything it stands for so for granted," she protested. "You and David always thought of it as something special, and really knew what it meant. But to me, it was just up there on a pole. I felt safe and happy when I saw it but I never thought about doing anything for it, the way David does."

"Well, you will now." Carrol pulled her through the crowd, and her eyes twinkled, although she said flatly: "You'll probably think again that you've just grown up."

They walked along, unmindful of the people jostling them, and only wishing they could see inside the square that had swallowed up the corps.

The lines had halted. "Ranks about face!" came the last command.

Again there was the thrill, the thump of rifles on the hard cement. The hot hands of the plebes were grasped by those of second classmen and the yearlings, and the stone square shook with voices. Mr. Dumbjohn was now dead! As a shrinking ghost he would haunt the Point until July, when other plebes would bring him to life again; but now the uniforms he once had filled were mingling with the other classes.

"Twenty minutes before we're due back at camp," David shouted above the noise, when the upper classmen had tired of the fun and had drifted away, and he and Michael were sauntering through the sally-port again. He waved to Penny and Carrol who were waiting in hot misery at an appointed place, and suggested, "How about a session in the Boodlers'?"

"Whoopee!" Penny left her small spot of shade and dragged Carrol with her. "Oh, happy day!"

They took the steps of Grant Hall in a bound and joined the shouting mobs around the tables. Those who were standing glared at the fortunate ones who were seated until the upper classmen gave up their places with a good-natured clap on the back for the plebes; and the Boodlers' resembled a fourth-class reunion.

"Isn't this marvelous?" Carrol asked as she peered at David over a cool iced drink.

"You bet. Are you happy?"

"I can't believe that any parade could have been so stirring. And I can't believe that we are actually sitting here, can you?"

"It's something I kept in mind all week when I ran my legs off and couldn't see you. Shall I come over home tonight for dinner?"

"Could you really come?"

"Sure." David's eyes met Michael's and Michael abandoned Penny and their laughing banter to lean across the table.

"Why, Dave," he said, "you aren't going to pass up supper with the chance to make some first classman hunt that gold-fish in the pitcher, are you?"

"Thought I would." David grinned at Carrol but she only frowned at him.

"David Parrish!" she cried. "You idiot, you'll do nothing of the kind. What happens tonight, Mike?"

She turned her head from David, and Michael was only too happy to explain. "We get the first classmen's seats and they get ours. If we have pie for dessert we can even throw it at 'em if we have a chance."

"Well, David's certainly going to have the chance. Coming over home, of all things!"

She smiled at David and wrinkled up her nose at him and he leaned back, at peace and satisfied. He tried to scowl at her and muttered something about its being a great thing when a girl didn't want him around, but his grin broke out and his fine effect was ruined.

"You're being stuffy," Penny accused him. "When you know you're simply dying to go to mess. In fact, now that you have had the satisfaction of sitting in this sacred spot I'll bet you're aching to get over to camp so that you can hob-nob with the second classmen."

"Well, we kind of are." Michael was honest in his answer. "But we'll be along to drag you to the hop tonight."

"And we'll be waiting." Carrol picked up the hat she had flung on the floor and set it on her head. "Come, my little yearlings," she said, "fish out your Boodlers' checks and let's by on our way."

"My soul, we haven't any, yet!" David looked at her blankly. "What do we do?"

"The ladies pay, of course." She shook some loose change from her pocket and the four heads bent over it to count the pennies and nickels and dimes.

"Please, could I have a candy bar?" Michael asked, clutching an extra five-cent piece. "I'm awful hungry and we'll never get a bite tonight."

"You can if you'll split it with David. Go on and get it."

"I can't use money." Michael laid the nickel down. "Do you want me up before the honor court tomorrow? You'll have to pay the check and bring the candy back."

"Such a place," Penny scolded as she scooped up the money and walked across to the counter. "Here." She poked the chocolate bar at Michael who had waited in the doorway and said, "I declare. I was so dewy-eyed and sentimental after the parade and felt that you were gods or something. Now I'm paying for your food!"

"Cheer up, my lamb," Michael teased her. "You'll be stepping on my feet tonight and I'll be much kinder to you than you are to me."

"I'll bet you will."

She and Carrol found their car and stood looking after the two erect figures that started their usual dog-trot down the street. They saw them stop, pound each other on the back, and go strolling off, as aimless and as debonair as though they had no immediate destination in mind.

"Dumbjohn or dumb-anything is a good name for us," David said, grinning as he let his shoulders slump. "You'd think we'd have sense enough to remember that we don't have to trot or hold ourselves like tent poles. Habit's a funny thing."

They went up and down the row of tents, found Dick and, when the bugle blew its mess call, marched happily across the plain. The line that met them came from barracks, and they smiled to watch first classmen scurrying from the ranks. The new gunners took their seats and the wary water corporals dodged the glasses that came flying at them. Fists beat on tables, Banshees howled, and from his poop deck up above, the watching officer was blind to a slap-stick comedy that featured custard pies.

For the first time in their eleven months of suffering, the plebes sat solidly upon their chairs and had a chance to see the dining hall. Dancing in the Thayer Hotel that night, while novel and exciting, was pale beside this feat.

"Even if it's graduation morning," Penny complained as she watched Faith and Denise laying dresses in their hand-trunks, "it's silly for you to go home this afternoon. The best fun is just beginning."

"I know it," Faith sighed as she rolled a wash dress around a pair of shoes, "but Mother and Father have some cock-eyed idea about a trip to the golden West. And of course Denise is all a-twitter over Steve's staying with them on Long Island. How was your romance last night, Dee?"

"Marvelous." Denise sat down on her trunk and reached under her for the clasps. "Steve's wonderful," she grunted as she tugged and pulled. "How was yours with Dick?"

"How would you think—with Dick?" The others laughed and Faith went on to explain. "I really had a whirl, but I laughed at the idiot from the time I got to the dance until he stepped all over my dress trying to open the screen door for me at home."

"Are you dragging him for Camp Illumination this summer?" Carrol chose a half of a cantaloupe from a large tray on the table and sat cross-legged on the bed.

"I suppose so. He muttered something about it—but after he ran me all the way home he had only five minutes to get into his little tent. Of course we got a late start from the hotel because he'd lost his cap, and when he tried to shake hands with me he only managed to knock my evening bag with all its contents off into space,—and the last I saw of him he was going down the hill at a dead gallop. He really is an entertaining soul."

"Poor Dick." Penny chose her breakfast, too, and fitted her back to the foot of the bed and the pillow Carrol tossed her. "He never has had much luck with girls. Which reminds me. . . ." Her fork paused halfway to her mouth. "Where was our dear *Louise?* I haven't seen her here."

"Who's she?" Faith's head came up and she was all attention.

"She's another gal from Arden," Penny answered. "Louise Frazier—or Lousie, if you care to change the spelling. She's in school somewhere and she nearly drove us crazy this winter. Praise be, I forgot to miss her."

Conversation centered on Louise, and Mary stumbling in from Camp Beauty Rest, yawned that Louise was back at Arden. "Dick said she didn't have a bid for June Week," she explained, pushing Penny over and curling up against the pillow. "I don't think I can ever make graduation exercises."

"You'll have to, pet." Penny offered her a slice of bacon. "Jonesy'll die if you aren't there to see him stand four hundred and forty-third in his class. How he got even nine files from the bottom is a mystery to me."

They took their time in dressing, and straggled into the Field House long after the corps was in its place. Graduates were receiving their diplomas, and the long line moved forward endlessly. Tired hands tried to be gracious with applause, but efforts were becoming feeble when the last man rose from his seat. Then the rafters shook with cheers and clapping. He was the "goat," the lowest in the class and a hero. Like the boy who stuck his finger in the dyke and held the flood, he had kept the class a solid structure—for without him it would have had no bottom.

When everything was still again, eighteen hundred cadets rose for the Long Corps, and four hundred and fifty-two of them who were cadets no longer, but young lieutenants in the Army, were solemn as their voices rang out for the last time "Y-E-A A-R-M-Y!"

"The new makes will be given out now," Penny said when

they were out in the sunshine. "The second classmen will be officers, the third class sergeants, and David's class the corporals. I hope he gets one."

"He will." They hurried to the plain where the three classes were assembled and Carrol, although she couldn't hear, watched and waited eagerly for them to break ranks.

"Yea furlough! Yea furlough!" The scattering second class cheered and threw caps into the air as its members dashed for barracks and the only summer vacation they would have in their four long years.

The road to Camp Clinton was crowded and Penny and Carrol, clinging together because of their common interest in two "wives," lost the other girls. They looked for Faith and saw her coming across the baseball field with Dick and Mary. She was talking earnestly to Dick, and Mary ran toward them.

"Don't say anything about corporals," she said breathlessly when she caught up with them. "Michael and David were made but Dick wasn't. He's trying to pretend he doesn't care, but he does. David says he'll get it in the fall."

"We won't mention it," they promised. But before Dick reached them he blurted it out himself.

"Fort Arden's in the money," he called. "I'm sorry I let her down."

"You didn't, Dick." Penny reached for him and linked her arm in his. "You'll make it later."

"David says you will." Carrol was on his other side and trying to smile comfort, too. "Don't worry about it, Dicky." She saw David coming and flew to meet him.

"Oh, David," she cried as their hands met. "I'm so proud!"

"Thanks, honey." David grinned and swung her hand in his. "You're dated up for a solid week," he told her. "We'll start it off with lunch at home, followed by a cooling swim at Delafield."

★

CHAPTER XVII

WEST POINT DREAMS

"The last one in the water is a tailless monkey," Dick shouted as he ran down the small beach at Delafield Pond.

He was his happy self again and his loss of promotion had ceased to trouble him. His feet touched the spring board and the crowd that jammed behind him sent him sprawling into the water. "My gosh, Mary," he cried as he spluttered up from the bottom of the lake, "for a hundred and fifteen pounds you can hit like a ton of dynamite."

David gave him another push and he went down again. They thrashed and churned the water in a battle that carried them to the float, and the others swam along behind.

The little lake, high up in the hills, was cool and tree-fringed. Groups were lying in the sun of a lazy afternoon, and the water was dotted with bright bobbing caps.

"This is the life," Michael said, swinging himself onto the float and reaching down for Penny. "That's some suit you're wearing, Miss America."

"It's brand new." Penny crawled up beside him, smoothed the red flounce that was meant to be a skirt and said with pride, "I bought it in Florida."

"That's not so new."

"It is for me, after that yellow rag I wore at Arden." She stretched a wet hand to Carrol who was swinging on the ladder. "What are you and David whispering about?" she asked.

"Nothing that concerns you, sister dear," David assured her. His elbows were on the float, his body trailed in the water. "We have an errand that we have to do in fifteen minutes."

"What?" Penny rolled to the edge and put her face close to his. "You're always doing things by minutes," she complained. "Fifteen minutes, twenty minutes—I should think you'd feel like an alarm clock."

"I do, sometimes. Okay, Carrol. Let's be on our way. We'll see you at the house."

They swam slowly to the bath house and dripped up the steps to its cement platform. "Make it snappy," David said when they parted for their dressing rooms.

"I'll hurry."

Carrol, in the dark as much as Penny, wondered where they were going. Her fingers fumbled annoyingly, a zipper caught and her hair tangled. At last she tied the belt around her green checked dress and snatched up her wet things. David was waiting in her car and she slid beneath the wheel. "Now where?" she asked.

"Drive down to Cullen first and I'll direct you."

They rolled down the slope, passing other swimmers coming up, and David lounged back in the seat, his half-smile hidden by his cap. He wore his school blouse again above white slacks and stretched his long legs before him.

"Once more, this reminds me of our first ride," Carrol remarked into his silence. "The day I sat in the car like so much excess baggage and tried to admire the Post and wished I'd never started out with you. I hope you haven't gone to sleep."

"Humhum." David looked at her and grinned. "Pull in this parking place," he directed, "and we'll start our trek."

"Our trek? You mean we're going to walk?"

"And how." David reached across her to swing her door open and they met at the back of the car. "All right, here we go."

They followed a tree-bordered path above the Hudson and suspicious thoughts stirred in Carrol's mind. When they reached a fork in the path she stopped and looked at David. "Oh yes, I thought so. It's Flirtation Walk," she said. "You were being mighty cagey, weren't you?"

David leaned against a tree and laughed. "Which way shall we go?" he asked.

"Well, glory, I don't know." Carrol thought with a shudder of the Kissing Rock. Tradition decreed that no girl must pass, unkissed, beneath it. Somewhere it hung, above one path or the other, solid in the cliff, and waiting to surprise a novice. She looked at David but he was only cocky against his tree. "Couldn't you decide?"

He shook his head. "Sorry, but that's for the girl to do."

She studied the paths again. The one to the right was smooth and shaded, the one to the left rose bumpily into the hill. What had Penny said one day? Something about. . . . Her mind searched frantically for Penny's words and she wished that sometimes her best friend weren't quite so voluble. Had Penny said, "Girls always take the smoothest way and then it's just too bad," or had she said . . . ?

"Well, what's it going to be?"

"Stop leering. You know you've got me on the spot." Once more she tried to coax her memory, then resorted to a childish trick. "Eeny, meeny, miney, moe," she counted with a wagging finger. The finger stopped on the level path and she surprised herself by saying: "I think I'll take the other one. I *know* that Penny said . . ."

"You're sure? You wouldn't like to change your mind?" The twinkle in David's eyes changed to a frown as he gave her another chance. "The other path looks nice."

"I'll choose the climb."

"All right, then. Here we go."

David gave her a starting shove and they walked on. The path dipped and turned and they followed its windings slowly.

Having safely solved the problem of the Kissing Rock, Carrol relaxed and David seemed to have forgotten it, too. He talked to her of his aspirations, just as he had at Arden, and when they rounded a bend, stopped to lean against another tree. "It's beautiful out here, isn't it?" he said, looking around him. "I'm glad I have the right to walk here now, and I'm glad you're the first girl I ever came with."

"I am, too. It's so still." Carrol lifted her head to listen to the soft whispering of the leaves and to watch a squirrel that chattered and frisked before them. He flirted his tail as he scampered along the path and Carrol's eyes followed him. At the base of a cliff he disappeared, and she stared at the spot where he had been. "What's that in front of us?" she gasped, "there, where the squirrel was?"

"What's what?" David looked at her instead of where she pointed, and the twinkle was back in his eyes.

"That thing—that rock that's sticking out."

There was no mistaking it. Kissing Rock, from all its pictures, hung before her. There it was. And here was David. And in order to get home she must walk with him beneath it. "You knew I'd taken the wrong path, didn't you?" she demanded. "That's why you're looking like the cat that ate the canary."

"I rather gathered that you had." David was mischievous as he looked at her flushed face.

"But I distinctly remember that Penny said . . ."

"There are two ends to this walk. Penny told you one and we came in the other."

"Oh." Carrol looked back along the path and put one foot behind her. "Shall we—shall we stroll back?" she suggested. "It was quite pretty along the way we came."

"A good soldier never retreats." David shook his head solemnly. "I'm learning to be a soldier and I'd feel pretty small if I let a little rock scare me."

"It isn't a little rock—it's a big one. And couldn't we just sort of—strategically, withdraw? Armies often do that."

David laughed. He took her hand and looked down at her. "You aren't the retreating kind, ever," he said. "So come on."

The distance to the rock was all too short. When they stepped under the roof it made, David tightened his hold and stopped her. "I bought you something," he said, pressing her fingers around a small white box. "I hope you'll want to keep it."

Carrol snapped open the cover. "Why, it's a pin," she breathed. "Oh, David!"

They both looked down at the small gold pin that was nestling on white velvet. Its A, that stood for *Army,* was pearl-encrusted, and three diamonds twinkled from its points.

"Oh, Davy!"

"Do you want to wear it?" His voice was shy but hopeful.

"You know I do." She took the pin from its box and opened the safety catch. "I'll never be without it," she promised as she slipped it into her dress above her heart.

She leaned against the cliff, and David took off his cap and turned it thoughtfully in his hands. "Three years from now we'll come here again," he said with a sigh, after having made a difficult decision, "and then I can say all the things I want to tell you now." He rested a hand on either side of her and looked down into her upturned face. "That doesn't seem so very long to wait, does it?"

"It isn't, Davy." Carrol's lips quivered as she looked up at him and he leaned forward and kissed them gently. Then he took her hand and they walked from beneath the rock's stern shadow and went slowly on.

The path dipped to the river and, as they scrambled down to the water's edge David asked, "Do you think a girl would mind being a second lieutenant's wife?"

"Of course not. She'd love it." Carrol waved to a little

boy who was standing at the rail of an excursion boat and David skipped a pebble into the water with the frowning intensity of a big league pitcher in a world series game.

"But there's practically no salary at all and she'd have to go hopping around the country and never be able to own a home. I'm talking about the kind of a girl who would live in a place like Gladstone," he said with a shy smile.

"So am I." She watched the little boy until he faded into a blur and her voice was placid when she said, "Your mother started out that way and she still likes it."

"I know she does." David skipped another pebble and watched the widening ring its ripples made. "But Mums is the happy contented kind who doesn't want to do big things or be important."

"Everything she does is very important to her." Carrol was emphatic in her answer. "She does big things, but you and Penny don't realize it because you both go around with your eyes on the stars." She smiled at him teasingly as she went on to explain. "I mean that you want to be a general and wear stars on your shoulders, and Penny wants to be an actress and have one painted on her dressing-room door."

"But you used to say that you wanted to do big and glorious things, too."

"I still do." She looked up at him and laughed. "But my ideas have changed. I love having you and Penny being ambitious and star-gazing, but perhaps . . ."

David looked deeply into the blue eyes that were smiling at him. "You're better off than either one of us," he said slowly, "because you have stars in your eyes."

"Thank you, Davy, dear." Carrol turned away from the river and from him to the shadows that were growing long. "It's getting frightfully late," she said with a practical sigh that quenched the stars. "It must be almost dinner time and Penny'll be having a fit. We'd better go."

Penny was having, if not a fit, a very trying time of sighs

and restlessness. "Where the dickens have Carrol and David gone?" she fumed as she roamed through the empty house.

Dick and Michael had long ago returned to camp, and Mary had gone to see her parents. Below her on the highway she could hear the steady stream of departing cars, and the voices of neighbors who were on their lawns calling last good-bys to guests. She wandered into Camp Beauty Rest, chaste and empty now, and finally threw herself on her own bed, pushing her lonely head into a pillow.

She was drowsing into much-needed rest when footsteps sounded on the stairs and Carrol tip-toed in. "Hi," Penny mumbled, opening one sleepy eye. "You must have had a long, long errand. Where's David?"

"He's downstairs, and going to stay for dinner." Carrol came to the foot of the bed and Penny lifted herself on an elbow.

She made no mention of the pin, so blatantly displayed, and Carrol wondered if she saw it. Penny's eyes that rarely missed a thing, were fastened on the window and she stretched luxuriously. "I've been doing a lot of thinking," she said, wriggling her toes in her stockings, "while you were all beasts enough to go off and leave me. And I've made some very fine decisions."

"What?" Carrol leaned on the low footboard of the bed, her new pin swinging four feet from Penny's nose. "What did you decide?"

"Well, first," Penny scrambled to reverse her position. "Just let me get comfortable." Her feet were on the pillow now and she had decreased her distance from the pin. Her eyes were dreamy as she looked off into space and Carrol waited impatiently for the shriek of discovery that she knew was bound to come.

"Go see what she says," David had urged. "I'd give a dollar to see her face when you walk in."

It wouldn't be worth a nickel, Carrol thought, waiting to

hear Penny's plans and trying not to show her disappointment.

"Well," Penny propped her chin up in her hands and kicked her heels, and said with great importance, "I was thinking about my future."

"Oh." Carrol forced a smile and Penny giggled. "I was having another conversation with my grandchildren."

"And I suppose you said, as usual, 'Darlings . . .'"

"You're quite right, I did." Penny shifted her pose once more, until she was sitting upright. Her feet were crossed beneath her and her impish face was close to Carrol's. "This time I said—now hold your breath because it's very different from any other time—this time I said, 'Darlings, Grandmother would never have become a famous actress if she hadn't gone to visit—at her *sister* Carrol's!'"

With a joyous little chuckle she reached out her arms and the pin was pressed between them.